MENTOR BOOKS

For the pupils in Scoil Cholmcille, Skryne

First Published 2005
by
MENTOR BOOKS
43 Furze Road,
Sandyford Industrial Estate,
Dublin 18.
Tel. (01) 295 2112/3   Fax. (01) 295 2114
e-mail: admin@mentorbooks.ie

ISBN: 1-84210-293-1

The Author
Originally from Stratford-on-Slaney,
Co. Wicklow, Kieran Fanning now lives
and works as a primary school teacher in Co. Meath.

Illustrations by Kieran Fanning
Design and layout by Kathryn O'Sullivan
Cover by Jon Berkeley
www.jonberkeley.com

Printed in Ireland by ColourBooks
1 3 5 7 9 10 8 6 4 2

Important Notice – Please read carefully!

This is not an ordinary book. You do not read straight through from beginning to end. Sam and Lisa need your help to solve puzzles and problems that occur in the story. The answer to a problem will lead you to the <u>next</u> page of the story. Sometimes you will have to turn to a **page number** but other times you will have to follow a **symbol**. These are the little pictures at the top left-hand corner of every left-hand page. All symbols and their page numbers are listed below.

You must solve the puzzles and problems <u>correctly</u> to find out the next page to turn to. If you are correct you will see the answer in bold print at the top of the page. If you are wrong you should go back and try again. If you get really stuck on any problem there is an answers page at the back of the book.

It might help to write down the page you are working on each time, so if you get the answer wrong you can go back and try again.

Good Luck!

				E							
2	4	6	8	10	12	14	16	18	20	22	24

					S						
26	28	30	32	34	36	38	40	42	44	46	48

50	52	54	56	58	60	62	64	66	68	70	72

W								N			
74	76	78	80	82	84	86	88	90	92	94	96

∅										V	
98	100	102	104	106	108	110	112	114	116	118	120

122	124	

. . . . symbols

. . . . page numbers

'So how come we never see your Uncle Dave?' pondered Lisa as she slouched over an armchair, flicking ferociously through the hundreds of channels that was 'American TV'. She didn't want to say it but it had been a bit boring staying with Sam's relations. After all, this was supposed to be a holiday.

Sam lifted his head. He knew only too well how Lisa felt because he felt it himself. But at least he had come to expect it. Every few years Sam and his mother visited Uncle Dave and Aunt Grace in Mexico and unless you were into going shopping with his mother and aunt, there wasn't that much to do. That's why he had invited his best friend Lisa to tag along this year.

'He has some big important job working for the government, doing research or something,' replied Sam.

'Oh?' said Lisa, flicking onto *Oprah*.

'He's an astronomer, I think. I don't really know. His work is top secret. That's why he never talks about it.'

Lisa sat up in the chair. 'Is that why we're not allowed in his study?'

'Probably.'

Lisa arched her eyebrows into a suggestion.

'No . . . we shouldn't,' warned Sam.

'Come on!' she shrieked, already racing out the door.

'Wait!' called Sam jumping up after her.

He chased her out the double doors and up the hall, turning left and then right. The third door on the left was open. Lisa had ignored the 'Do not enter' sign.

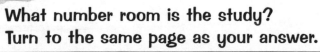

What number room is the study?
Turn to the same page as your answer.

Four words is the correct answer.

Artox reappeared at the door, beckoning Lisa into the control room where Blats continued to monitor screens and work on computers.

Artox directed Lisa to an empty chair.

'If the only way you'll return to Earth willingly is with your friends, then we must rescue them before they're infected.'

Lisa smiled her first smile on Blattaria.

'The problem is going to be getting into The Tower where they are held prisoner. Although we have some spies inside, none of them is capable of, or willing enough, to pull off this rescue.'

'Taking an air buggy is too risky,' said another Blat. 'Perimeter radar will pick it up.'

'And ground entrances are heavily guarded,' added another.

To Lisa they were ignoring the obvious solution.

'Why not just fly in?' she blurted. 'You've all got wings.'

All the Blats looked at her blankly. What had she said?

A Blat called Croy eventually stood up and showed her his back.

'Blattarian law states that all Blats must keep their wings cut. Failure to do so is punishable by death. Only those inside The Tower and the guards are allowed to fly. Another way of controlling the masses.'

'Looks like ground entry is our best bet,' continued Artox.

'Sneak in by cover of day then,' added another.

Again it was Croy who noticed Lisa's confusion.

'Blats sleep during the day. The light hurts our eyes.'

'Any update on the location of the humans?' demanded Artox from a Blat at a computer screen.

'No sir. Still no word from the first rescue team either.'

'There's no time to waste,' urged Artox, spreading a map out on the table. 'Let's look for the entrance that's least guarded.'

'Sentry posts,' reminded Croy, 'are marked with the letter S.'

START HERE

S

S

S

S

S

S

S

74

14

40

32

The
Tower

48

S

S

22

S

S

S

S

S

OR HERE

It's possible to reach one of the entrances
without passing any sentry posts. Which one?
Turn to the same page as your answer.

Floor six is the correct answer.

'Stand still,' advised Dajus before hitting a green button.

The teleporter powered up. Lisa felt instantly light-headed, light-bodied too, as if she was floating. She looked at Artox. He was fading quickly. As was Dajus. They looked like ghosts.

Lisa glanced down at her own body. It too was growing dim. She was disappearing bit by bit, particle by particle. She looked back at the Blats. They were almost gone – and then there was nothing. Nothing but white light. No Dajus, no Artox, no Lisa.

And then a shape materialised, an outline, hazy and without colour but growing more defined. It was a creature. Two in fact. It was Artox and Dajus. Now Lisa became aware of her own body, filling up, taking shape, reappearing.

In seconds she was whole again, as were the two Blats, all standing together once again in the teleporter. Everything was exactly the same.

'Wh . . . what happened?' stuttered Lisa.

'We've just been teleported to level six,' replied Dajus.

'But . . . ' began Lisa looking around.

'All the teleporters look the same,' said Dajus returning to the keypad. 'It's just a pity we can't teleport directly to the top. These blasted cargo routes only go up five levels or down two. There aren't cargo teleporters on every level but we'll go as high as we can.'

He keyed in another number and pressed the green button.

Here we go again, thought Lisa, already feeling her body dissolving.

What's the highest level that they can reach?
Turn to the same page as your answer.

= cargo teleporter

Air buggy number eight is the correct answer.

Artox eased off the throttle, allowing the guards to sail past. One waved and shouted something. Artox casually returned the greeting.

Lisa popped out her head. The Tower loomed in front of them, obliterating everything else from their field of vision. It was truly enormous. She watched the guards who had just flown past disappear into various entrances high up in The Tower.

'We cannot fly any further,' announced Artox. 'The perimeter radar will pick up the identity of this buggy and the craft will automatically switch to auto-pilot. It will then be guided automatically to whichever station it belongs to. Security precautions.'

Although she was listening, Lisa was still mesmerised by The Tower and its thousands of windows.

'Hold on!' shouted Artox, as he manoeuvred the buggy into a steep descent.

They were still a long way from The Tower when the machine landed in the desert on the outskirts of it. Lisa peered up at the gigantic building. It was so high that the top of it couldn't be seen.

'The Tower,' said Artox, jumping out of the air buggy, 'is surrounded by a high wall. Ground access is only possible through one of the gates. Many of the gates themselves aren't guarded but unfortunately, the area surrounding The Tower is heavily dotted with Blattarian Guard sentry posts. We have a maze of sentry posts to negotiate before we even get to a gate. Only thing on our side is that it's daytime.'

Lisa remembered the Blats plotting the best route on a map back in BUG's headquarters. She slid off her backpack to check if Kreeia had given her a copy.

Look again at the map on page 5.
Which of the gates on <u>this</u> page should they
set out for?
To return to Sam, turn to the same page as the
symbol on the gate.

Room number ten is the correct answer.

The doors hissed apart and two Blats entered, wearing white masks over their entire heads. The masks allowed the creatures' antennae to poke out and had a filtered section for breathing through. Their eyes were shielded by a dark panel. They approached the children and took a syringe each. Almost simultaneously, they held the needles up to the light as if to examine them.

The doors suddenly hissed open again. Sam didn't know whether to look at the syringe that loomed dangerously overhead, or at the Blat who had just entered. But it wasn't a Blat. Although its face couldn't be seen because it too wore a white mask, it was definitely human. Sam knew by the hands. He knew by the walk. He knew by the lab coat. He knew his Uncle Dave.

Come to supervise, thought Lisa.

A claw suddenly pushed her sleeve up. Sam's sleeve was also pushed up to reveal his wrist and the veins running down into his hand. All he could do was scream. Lisa joined in, and their wailing penetrated the electronic door. Even the guards outside shuddered at the sound. When the screeching abruptly ended, they knew the job was done.

Inside, however, the scene was quite different from what they were imagining. The reason the screaming had ended was not because the children had been injected with a deadly virus, but because the two Blats who had been about to administer the disease had been shot dead. They lay, along with their deadly syringes, in a tangled heap on the floor between Sam and Lisa's beds.

Sam looked up. His uncle was coming towards him wielding a laser gun. When he arrived by his side he took off his mask. It wasn't his uncle. It was Professor Snyde!

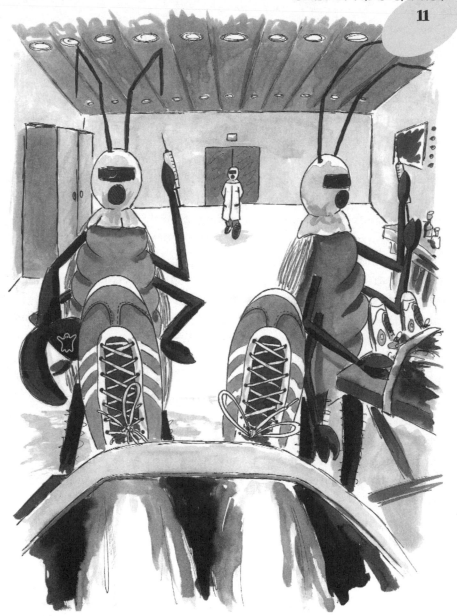

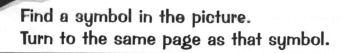

Find a symbol in the picture.
Turn to the same page as that symbol.

CURSE OF THE COCKROACH

12

The tent symbol is the correct answer.

Artox led the way towards the gate. He dropped down on all six limbs and scuttled along the ground. It was the first time that Lisa really saw the cockroach in him. She watched him scurry for cover to one of the many buildings that dotted the surrounding desert. Some of the buildings were new sentry posts, while others were obviously the shells of old ones. Hunching, Lisa followed the Blat. Inside the building crackled a strange language on either a radio or television.

'Best go separately,' whispered Artox. 'If we run into a guard, at least we won't both be caught.'

He scurried off at amazing speed, zigzagging between the cover of buildings. The hum of an air buggy suddenly filled the air and Lisa pressed herself in against the building. She watched it disappear over The Tower wall. When the coast was clear, she ran after Artox, her two feet matching the rate of her heart. Although it was giant insects that she was fearful of, it was she who felt like one, scampering recklessly across the desert like a spider across a living room floor.

She spotted Artox at the gate and made for him. Wearing the helmet, he looked exactly like a Blattarian guard. His ragged wings, however, reminded her that he wasn't.

Artox had removed a panel on the wall and was examining a tangle of wires.

'One of these buttons opens the gate,' he explained. 'The others set off an alarm.'

Which button opens the gate?
Turn to the same page as your answer.

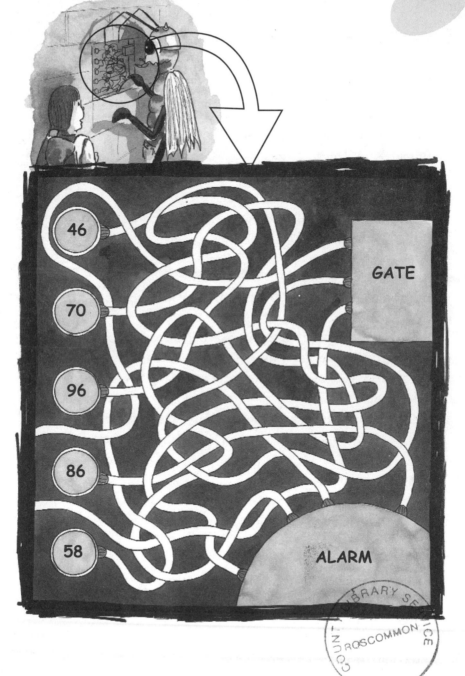

Entrance fourteen is the correct answer.

'I think a lone Blat operation is most likely to succeed,' announced Artox.

The other Blats agreed.

'I'm going to do it,' he revealed.

'But sir . . . What if . . . '

'If something happens, Croy takes over. Of all our missions, this one is paramount.'

Lisa decided it was time to speak.

'I'm going with you,' she said.

Artox shook his head.

'No you're not. It's too risky.'

'But Sam and Dave won't trust you. They may not go willingly. But if you have me . . . '

'She's right, sir,' Croy interrupted, 'but there is a better reason to take her. If you have her with you, then you can go straight for the teleporter once you've rescued the others. It'll save you returning here to pick her up.'

Artox was silent for a long time. Finally he nodded in agreement.

'It'll be daytime soon,' he said. 'Once light descends, we will set off.'

'Yes sir!' shouted the Blats.

'Frizleck, download any plans, blueprints and access codes for The Tower onto my MDU. Anything you've got, I want it.'

'Yes sir!'

'And Kreeia . . .'

A Blat with a missing antenna stepped forward.

'Take the girl and hook her up with a micro-com, a laser and anything else she might need.'

'Yes sir!' replied the Blat in a voice which was definitely female.

'Go with Kreeia,' said Artox to Lisa.

Which Blat is Kreeia?
Turn to the same page as your answer.

Sixteen is the sum of the five numbers in the message.

'Is this exciting or what!' chirped Sam. His eyes were wide and he wore a grin that most boys his age were normally too cool to wear. Lisa on the other hand, looked more like Sam normally looked, serious and sombre.

'I think we should go find your uncle,' she said. 'He's been gone a long time.'

Lisa led the way back down the metal balcony. She stopped at a door in the wall. As she leaned forward to push it, the door hissed open automatically. A pale tiled corridor invited them to another door at the far end.

'Are you sure it's this way?' asked Sam a little apprehensively.

Lisa nodded and headed for the door at the end of the corridor. It too hissed open but it was dark inside. Sam stood under the sensor while Lisa explored within. She felt along the wall and found a light switch. The room flickered into brilliance.

Lisa's sudden gasp brought Sam immediately to her side. He saw what had startled her. A pool of fresh blood lay on the white floor. Blood had been dragged from the pool, across the tiles, disappearing under a door on the opposite wall. A length of timber lay suspiciously nearby.

Sam looked fearfully at his friend. His excitement had quickly evaporated and was replaced by an escalating sense of terror. The worst part was that both children knew they couldn't give in to their instinct to flee. They knew they had to keep going.

Sam glanced around. A computer, shelves, documents, coils of wire and boxes adorned the walls but his eyes were inevitably drawn back to the door with the blood under it.

He walked over and tried the handle. It was locked. There was an electronic keypad on the wall. Three of the buttons were covered in blood.

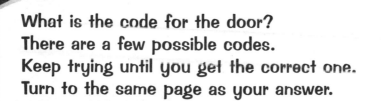

What is the code for the door?
There are a few possible codes.
Keep trying until you get the correct one.
Turn to the same page as your answer.

CURSE OF THE COCKROACH

Building number eighteen is the correct answer.

As Lisa moved through the giant insect infested streets, she was amazed to find that nobody took any notice of her. Nor was she the only one dressed up as a spectre. Many other 'ghosts' like herself floated about inconspicuously.

In fact she was glad she was under a sheet because it meant that she could hold her nose to stop herself from gagging at the wicked smell. Many of the creatures looked sick or dying, slumped in doorways or coughing on the street. That was the smell, she realised. The smell of death.

Others were crippled or injured, missing legs or arms or eyes or antennae. All of them had stunted, ragged wings, except for the guards who had immaculately long, silky ones draped down their backs. These wings, however, were not just for show as Lisa saw when a guard in front of her leapt up into the sky and flew off into the night. Anything that wasn't a guard trudged miserably along the ground.

The presence of the guards was blatant. They patrolled the area with authority and power, instilling fear and servitude in the other creatures. Many of them flew overhead, surveying the walkways below.

Lisa moved steadily along the narrow streets, trying to remember the directions. Although she didn't know where she was going, she would be glad to get in off the streets.

She made the final turn and found herself at the door of a mud house. Stepping inside, she found it empty except for a burning torch which cast spritely shadows on the floor. Something moved on the wall. It was a curtain covering a doorway. Lisa pulled it back and was surprised to find a very modern looking metal door. The door was covered in buttons, each marked with a letter. It looked like a giant word search.

To open the door find a word in the word search.
Turn to the same page as that symbol.

The cockroach symbol is the correct answer.

When Artox reappeared, Lisa questioned him.

'Surely cockroaches couldn't have survived an atomic war?'

'They could and they did,' replied Artox, sitting down. 'Didn't they survive the atomic bombing of Hiroshima and Nagasaki on your own planet?'

Lisa frowned at the Blat. 'How come you know so much about Earth?'

Artox stood up and gestured towards the door.

'Come and I'll show you.'

He opened the door back into the control room. Lisa stepped inside. Artox pointed to a screen that one of the Blats was watching. Lisa peered at it. Could it be true? They were watching television broadcast from Earth! One Blat was watching a Japanese documentary, another was watching a French film and another was watching an early episode of *The Simpsons*.

'Radio waves,' explained Artox, leading Lisa back into the other room. 'They travel forever through space. You just need the right equipment to pick them up. Unfortunately it takes years for the waves to travel here, so we're a bit behind on the news.'

'You mean you've been listening to us and watching us for years?' Lisa asked, disbelievingly.

'Well yes, even though it's illegal.'

'And what if you get caught?'

'More than a white sheet, I'm afraid.'

'White sheet?'

'Oh yes,' laughed Artox. 'I should have explained. Minor offences are punishable by having to wear a white sheet for a day, a week or even a month. Torturous for a Blat to have his antennae covered.'

Suddenly becoming serious again, he pointed to the pages on the table. 'You really need to finish this.'

Being the only living thing left on Blattaria, the cockroaches faced their greatest challenge. Of course, many died of radiation, but those that survived gave birth to a new species of super-bug, which was immune to and eventually thrived on radiation.

It's the law of nature that when a species faces a challenge, it evolves to overcome it. The reason that cockroaches are one of the only creatures on Earth that haven't evolved is because they haven't needed to. They have always had enough to eat and drink, and with the arrival of humans and their dustbins, they now have more than enough.

On Blattaria however, they needed to evolve. Only the strongest, biggest, most intelligent creatures survived. They gave birth to a stronger, bigger, more intelligent generation, who in turn did the same. This happened over millions of years, until the cockroach had evolved into a Blat, five to seven feet tall, standing upright, highly intelligent and with the ability to reason, imagine and speak.

Civilisation developed for a second time on Blattaria. Archaeologist Blats discovered the history of their planet, the history of the humans who had once lived there and the history of the technology that eventually destroyed them. Scientist Blats improved on this technology and turned Blattaria into a highly developed technological planet. We have created things that Earthlings can only dream about.

Follow the gun symbol.

Read the above page.
You will be told to follow a symbol.
To find out what happened to Sam, turn to the same page as that symbol.

Twenty-two minutes is the correct answer.

The bus doors hissed open inhaling hot dry Mexican air and perspiring customers. The children were glad to be back under air conditioning. Lisa gazed out the bus window. Having read that e-mail, she now understood why Sam's uncle had returned to work last night.

He had arrived home late, sat down, had a cup of tea with his wife and Sam's mother, played two video games with herself and Sam, gone to his study and returned minutes later with his jacket in hand.

'Crisis at work,' he had announced.

Sam's aunt hadn't seemed surprised. In fact, she hadn't reacted at all.

'I promise I'll do something fun with you tomorrow,' he had said, smiling at Sam and Lisa before rushing out the door.

Lisa liked Sam's Uncle Dave and, even though she had only seen him a few times since they had arrived, he always seemed to be in a good mood, laughing or joking about something. Most of her own uncles were as grumpy as anything.

'It must be very lonely for your Aunt Grace with your uncle working all the time,' she remarked turning to Sam.

'Why do you think she likes shopping so much!'

Sam didn't know that much about his uncle. In fact nobody did. He lived a sort of secret life but popped in and out of other peoples' lives full of enthusiasm and radiance. Uncle Dave always remembered things that you told him: what age you were, what you liked, what you didn't, and he never forgot your birthday. Most adults weren't like that, especially uncles.

The bus slumped to a halt.

'Rancho El Preson,' called the driver.

Sam and Lisa jumped out onto a crowded square.

Sam's Uncle Dave (white lab coat and briefcase!) was easily spotted among the local Mexicans.

Which number person is Uncle Dave?
Turn to the same page as your answer.

Location twenty-four on the map is the correct answer.

The first thing Lisa noticed was that it was night-time. She looked up into the sky in bewilderment. Through a high, metal-meshed dome, she could see distant stars.

'Get in quick!' whispered the smaller of the two creatures.

They were sitting in a small vehicle with a cage on the back, the gate of which swung open. Lisa obeyed without thinking.

'Now pull the gate.'

She did so and heard the lock click. The vehicle hummed softly and then quite suddenly jolted into the air, throwing Lisa to the floor.

'Sorry,' whispered the driver. 'I'm out of practice.'

Lisa pulled herself upright and looked out. The vehicle was slowly rising up into the air. Below she could see the hexagonal platform and the dome-shaped machine that looked strangely familiar.

She looked up: they were trapped beneath the metal-meshed roof! As they approached it, however, she noticed a small sentry box attached to the mesh. Inside sat two creatures who nodded in recognition at the driver. An electronic gate slid back to reveal a hole leading out to the black sky. As they cruised through the opening, the guards stared at her. As soon as they were out, their aircraft raced across the night sky. It was only then that Lisa really began to worry.

Where are they taking me? Why should I trust these vile beasts? I saw what they are capable of. I must escape!

It was all she could think of. She looked at the lock on the gate and then at the strange bunch of keys on the floor.

Which key will open the lock?
Turn to the same page as your answer.

Inside of Lock

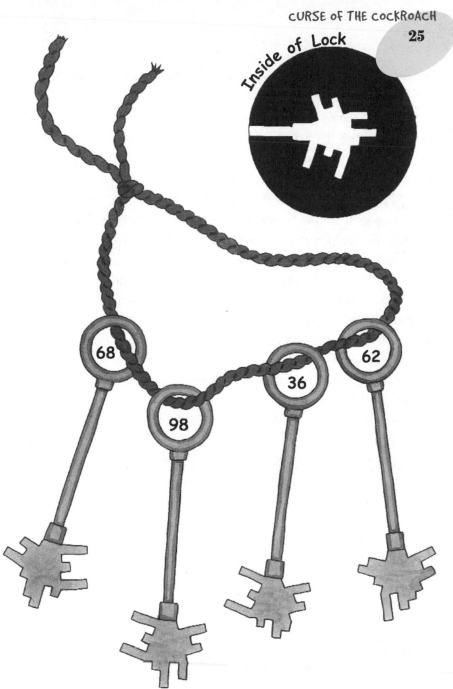

Twenty-six sticks of dynamite is the correct answer.

They placed the dynamite inside the teleporter, under the satellite dish and in each of the buildings on the mountain top. Each stick was attached to a fuse and all were connected to a long wire which the professor unrolled from a large coil.

'What about the rest of the workers?' asked Lisa, as the professor backed away from the explosives, unrolling the wire as he went.

'Once the teleporter was built, the staff was scaled down to myself, Dave and a few others.'

'And nobody knew about Blattaria's plan to colonise Earth?'

'Nobody except Dave. The Blats have been communicating with us for twenty years, supposedly for the purpose of forming a friendly alliance between the two planets. That's why we built the teleporter. It seems that they were also communicating privately with Dave. Only he was aware of their real intentions. Why he was prepared to sell Earth to these monsters, I still don't understand.'

'Power,' replied Lisa. 'They promised to make him ruler of this whole planet.'

They stopped in a small cluster of five trees. The professor had cut the wire and was connecting it to a detonator.

'I only discovered Dave's secret agenda by accident when I went into his office to look for a manual. He wasn't there but I decided to look for it anyway. I didn't think he would mind.'

Professor Snyde stopped talking and raised the handle on the detonator. 'Cover your ears,' he warned.

He looked up at the distant teleporter one last time before plunging the handle.

48

30

118

58

8

In which area of the mountain top are the professor and the children?
If you don't know, read page 26 again.
Turn to the same page as your answer.

Two, eight were the correct co-ordinates to enter on the keypad.

The shot was on target and the buggy tumbled out of the sky in a stream of smoke. Sam scanned the clouds for the other one. The sky was empty except for The Tower which was now rapidly retreating into the horizon. He turned around to locate the rest of their group only to find the second Blattarian guard tailing the buggy occupied by the single BUG soldier. The guard had lined himself up behind it and released a bolt of white light into the back of it. The buggy tumbled forward before spiralling out of control towards the ground.

The guard then proceeded to chase Lisa's craft. Sam whirled the gun around and studied the screen. Sam's pilot immediately understood and picked up speed to get them closer. Once again Sam's first shot missed but his second was on target and sent the enemy buggy reeling helplessly towards the desert below.

Lisa, who had watched the buggy chase with a strange feeling of both terror and exhilaration, gave her friend a thumbs-up. She and the professor smiled as they received one back. Then they turned their attention to the ground below. They had long since left The Tower behind and were crossing the arid desert. Signs of life, however, were beginning to show. A single mud hut quickly became two or three, and then many. Soon the entire ground below them was crammed with shacks around which a few early risers moped. Night was descending on the slums. Lisa searched for the teleporter.

Can you see the teleporter?
What number is it?
Turn to the same page as your answer.

Ladder number thirty is the correct answer.

The shafts up through The Tower walls were unlit and Lisa wondered how the Blats could see where they were going. She then remembered that it was the light and not the darkness that they had trouble with. As she ascended a ladder in pitch darkness, she was glad to have Dajus above her and Artox below.

Her legs were getting tired and each time they entered another level's maintenance tunnel, she hoped that it would be the last. But there was always another ladder.

All right for you Blats, she thought, with your long muscular legs and extra set of arms. She was about to voice her concerns when Dajus' voice echoed down the shaft. It was like music to her ears.

'This should be level 56!'

Lisa emerged into the maintenance tunnel of level 56. Her energy levels surged with the thoughts that Sam and Dave were somewhere nearby.

'This level is Tower Storage,' informed Dajus, heading down the tunnel. 'It's used to store important government items as well as possessions from high-level Blats. The floor is uninhabited, which is why it's a good place to hide. This is where I left your friend, the adult Earthling.'

'And what about Sam?' demanded Lisa.

'One at a time,' said Dajus.

He pushed open a door and entered the storage area. They were on a balcony overlooking a vast area crammed with boxes and crates and bags and many other strange objects. Dajus scanned the floor below.

'I told him not to move,' he muttered to himself angrily.

Even under the dim lights, it was Lisa's eyes which proved to be the sharpest. She could see him. She could see Sam's Uncle Dave!

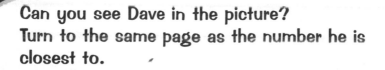

Can you see Dave in the picture?
Turn to the same page as the number he is
closest to.

Glove was the word in the word search.

Behind the door, a row of steps led underground. At the bottom of them waited the taller of the two creatures who had rescued her.

'We knew that you'd be able to open the door,' it said. 'It probably didn't look like much of a lock to you but very few up there speak English and even fewer know your alphabet. Follow me.'

They continued down a dark tunnel into a room full of activity. Half a dozen creatures or more sat around computers and screens, busy at work. They all stared at Lisa as she entered. Lisa's guide snapped an order in some strange language and everybody returned to work. She was then brought to a quieter room and sat down at the table.

'What's your name?' the creature asked.

'Lisa.'

'You looked a little horrified when you first saw me, and that's understandable. We, however, know all about humans and have been studying you for years, but you know nothing about us, so here goes.

'You are on planet Blattaria in the Eagle Nebula, billions of kilometres from your planet, Earth. I am a Blattarian, or Blat for short. All the creatures you have seen are Blats. We are the highest life form on our planet just as you are on yours. My name is Artox and I am the leader of this group of Blats. We call ourselves BUG – Blattarian Underground Guerrilla and we—'

The door opened.

'Message from The Tower, sir,' said the Blat at the door.

'Excuse me,' apologised Artox, rising from the table. 'Here, we've made out a short history of our planet to help you understand things.'

He motioned to some sheets of paper on the table and then left the room. On top of the pages lay a small mirror.

Earthlings

When life on Blattaria was beginning, your planet, Earth, didn't even exist. Life began on Blattaria the same way as it began on Earth: land and oceans, then bacteria, then insects and fish and reptiles, and, eventually, mammals and people. Blattaria is billions of years older than Earth.

When single-celled organisms started appearing on Earth, Blattaria already had civilisation, cities and technology. We had a massive head start. Millions of years ago, our planet looked very like yours looks today.

From excavation, we also know quite a bit about the people who lived on Blattaria, their history, their empires, their wars, their lives. In fact, they looked quite like Earthlings.

Much of what we learned doesn't concern you. Except for one artefact. It was of no value to those who made it but is priceless to our Blattarian government.

Ask Arfox about it.

Now follow the apple symbol.

Read the contents of the first page.
You will be told to follow a symbol.
Turn to the same page as that symbol.

The fish symbol is the correct answer.

The Blat who had called himself Dajus, retrieved his gun and joined Dave outside the cell.

'Hello kids!' grinned Dave.

Sam gaped at his uncle in horror. Lisa stared at the body of the dead Blat.

'Sorry about your friend,' Dave said to her. 'It couldn't be helped. I didn't spend half of my lifetime on this project only to have it ruined by some do-gooder cockroach.'

The Blat snorted disapprovingly.

'I mean Blat,' apologised Dave, 'some do-gooder Blat. Now, get these two up to the government boardroom. They're waiting on us. We've wasted enough time already.'

'Yes sir,' replied the Blat.

Sam could hear his uncle walking away, while the Blat uttered some gibberish command into a claw-held device. The creature then removed a small vial of liquid from his belt, flipped open a compartment on his gun and placed it inside. He snapped it shut again and pressed a button on the side of the weapon as he pointed it at Sam.

Sam looked frantically at Lisa and then back at the gun. He watched the claw pull the trigger. He heard the whoosh of something shooting through the air and then felt a piercing sting in his shoulder. Suddenly his vision began to go. Everything became cloudy and dim. He heard the gun go off again and a sharp gasp from Lisa. As darkness closed in he could just make out the shapes of other bodies entering the room and then everything went black.

Find a symbol in the picture.
Turn to the same page as that symbol.

The S symbol is the correct answer.

Lisa eased her eyelids open. Bright light flooded in, blinding and hurting her eyes. She squinted for some relief. While her retinas adjusted to the light, she became aware that she couldn't move. Her hands and feet were clamped firmly in place. Gradually her sight returned, revealing her prison.

She was standing up but shackled to a wall inside a glass capsule. The capsule was in a cylindrical room. Attached to the walls were five more capsules and there were people in two of them! Opposite her was Sam's Uncle Dave. He too was manacled standing up, except that he was either asleep or unconscious or . . .

Lisa turned her head to the capsule beside her. It was Sam. He was struggling to free himself but to no avail. When he saw her he started to shout but she couldn't hear him. All she could do was stare back helplessly.

Things, however, were about to get a lot worse. Lisa watched in horror as a green gas began pouring into the bottom of Sam's capsule, slowly filling it up. She could see the terror in Sam's eyes as he began coughing and choking for air. In seconds the gas had engulfed him and when it cleared Lisa saw his head was hanging limply to one side and his eyes were closed, just like his Uncle Dave.

Lisa's panic reached boiling point. She screamed and pulled frantically at her steel manacles but already the gas was coiling around her feet. It took only seconds to fill the glass chamber and bring an end to her screams.

Find a symbol in the picture.
Turn to the same page as that symbol.

Zero, three, eight is the correct code for the door.

The children stepped into a factory of some sort. All around them were machines of every shape and size, all connected to each other via pipes and cables and conveyor belts. And yet it was eerily silent. They felt as if they had just stepped into a cage full of sleeping metal monsters. One wrong foot and they might all wake up whirring, grinding and spitting with rage.

Sam scanned the warehouse. There were doors on every wall and, high above, a metal-meshed walkway with even more doors ran right around the perimeter of the warehouse.

Had it not been for the blood trail, they surely would have lost their way. The trail, however, was fading with every step and the concrete floor of the factory made it difficult to follow. The blood was soaking into the porous ground, leaving only dark blotches instead of scarlet stains.

The children followed the trail through the maze of machines and past long tables covered in drawings and blueprints. They eventually arrived at large metal double doors, like those of an elevator. Another electronic keypad seemed to be the only means of opening them. This time however, there were no blood marks on the buttons.

Sam tried the same code that had worked on the last door. A negative buzz told him it was too good to be true.

Lisa was examining a notice board on a nearby wall. Tacked onto it were many messages.

Can you find the code for the elevator?
Turn to the same page as your answer.

Dear workers,
You will all have received your redundancy letters by now. Let us once again take this opportunity to thank you for all your work at SARC. Unfortunately funding for the project has ended and therefore the experiment has been cancelled. You are asked to remove all your possessions by next Tuesday. Your keys and remote controls will be collected from you then.

Let us remind you that the confidentiality clauses that you signed remain legally binding even after you have left here.
Yours sincerely,
Board of Directors, SARC

The teleporter has been deemed unsafe. Still OK to use for messaging.

Door on storage shed beside satellite dish is not very secure. Needs re-enforcement.

Finishing up party in Digger's house tonight 8 p.m.

Last set of instructions due this week!

Dear Dave,
The teleporter reads that a message was received last night but there is no sign of one. This is not the first time that this has happened. Either the messages are being collected by someone else or the teleporter is faulty.
Brian Clarke,
Chief Engineer

COMPUTER FOR SALE. Contact Conor McGuinness.

Teleporter seems to be malfunctioning. Again it reads that new message received but no message inside.

LAST PERSON OUT PLEASE REMEMBER TO LOCK WAREHOUSE DOOR

New code for elevator: 106

SEAN COWAN – YOU STILL OWE MONEY FOR COFFEE!

Hey guys, I think Snyde has a girlfriend. Heard him on the phone last night!

Dear Brian,
RE: Security camera action
Sorry Brian that was me last night that set off the alarm. I left something up at the teleporter and just went back to get it. Nothing to worry about.
Prof. Snyde

Number forty was the number that Dave was closest to.

Ignoring Dajus who reached out a restraining claw, Lisa raced down the stairs into the storage area. She found an equally jubilant Dave, waiting for her with outstretched arms. As she fell into his welcoming embrace, tears nearly overwhelmed her, and they probably would have were it not for the many questions that she needed to ask.

'How did you escape?' she uttered.

Dave nodded over her shoulder.

'Dajus here rescued me. He's an undercover agent for some revolutionary movement, BUG, I think it's called.'

Lisa nodded excitedly and introduced Dave to the other Blat.

'This is Artox, the leader of BUG. He rescued me!'

Dave went to shake hands but changed his mind and spoke instead.

'Thank you Artox, and although I am extremely grateful to you both, I am also extremely worried about my nephew, Sam.'

'He's locked up in one of the holding cells, ten levels up,' said Dajus. 'I can bring him here.'

'I'm coming with you,' announced Lisa firmly.

'Fine,' said Dajus, 'but we must hurry.'

'If the girl goes, then I must go,' added Artox.

'No,' retorted Dajus firmly. 'The less of us there are, the less chance of being spotted.'

Reluctantly, Artox agreed, and Dajus headed to a nearby cargo teleporter.

'We'll be back as soon as we can.'

Lisa looked at Dave. He smiled and gave her a thumbs-up. She could sense that he was proud of her. Even Artox bowed his head as a sign of respect for the young girl.

She turned on her heels and followed the Blat to the teleporter.

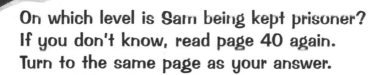

On which level is Sam being kept prisoner?
If you don't know, read page 40 again.
Turn to the same page as your answer.

Room number forty-two is the correct answer.

'Get a load of this!' marvelled Lisa as Sam entered the room.

Each wall of the study was lined with books, thousands of them, from floor to ceiling. A small writing desk was covered with papers, and a computer built into the bookshelves hummed softly.

'We shouldn't be in here,' warned Sam as Lisa ran her index finger along the book spines.

'*Alien Encounters, A New Species, UFOs, Alien Abductions – Survivor Stories, Area 51 – The Cover Up* . . . He's not your average uncle is he?' she said, plonking herself down in front of the computer.

'Don't touch it,' said Sam. 'He'll know we were in here.'

Lisa moved the mouse and the dancing aliens screensaver disappeared. On screen was an e-mail.

```
Dave
I think we need to talk. And don't even think about
phoning. I want to speak to you face to face.
Immediately. Come to my office.
Prof. Snyde
```

Lisa leaned back in the chair and scanned the books overhead.

'Well, I don't know what your uncle does or who he works for, but I'd rather him than me.'

Suddenly a phone rang in the study. Sam jumped.

'Jeeez . . .' he muttered, his heart galloping in his chest.

Lisa laughed at him.

'Well aren't you going to answer it?'

'I would if I could find it!'

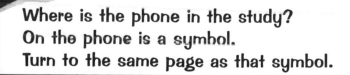

Where is the phone in the study?
On the phone is a symbol.
Turn to the same page as that symbol.

Speaker number forty-four was Dajus.

The iron doors parted and the cart crawled nervously into The Tower. After a short journey, the vehicle stopped and Dajus removed the canvas sheet. Lisa and Artox saw a gigantic ceiling soaring above them. Its clean geometric lines and gleaming metals were a sharp contrast to the grimy murkiness of the outside slums.

Climbing out, they were faced with an even more dazzling sight. The whole base of The Tower spread out before them. It was truly enormous, the size of a small town. Hundreds of metallic domes covered the floor like haystacks in a meadow.

'No time to give you the guided tour,' whispered Dajus. 'We need to get you to a teleporter. There are four on this level but security down here is tight. Do you see those tiny flashing lights on the outside of each dome?'

Artox nodded.

'They're sensors. They track the movement of all Tower Blats by reading a microchip in their skulls. I have one but you don't. If you pass between any of them, the alarm will sound. I'm going to try to shut down some of the sensors for a few minutes. As soon as you see the lights turn off, run to whichever teleporter you can reach. Wait for me there and remember, do not pass between any active sensors.'

Dajus disappeared into the maze of domes. Lisa focused on the flashing sensors. She tuned everything else out. She tuned out the strange surroundings. She tuned out the thousands of questions that were burning holes in her brain. She even tuned out her pounding heart. She was ready to run.

Two of the nearby sensors suddenly stopped flashing. That was Lisa's starting pistol.

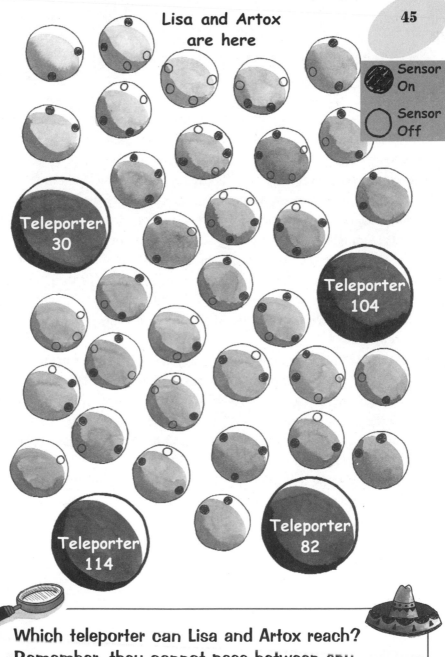

Lisa and Artox
are here

Sensor
On

Sensor
Off

Teleporter
30

Teleporter
104

Teleporter
114

Teleporter
82

Which teleporter can Lisa and Artox reach?
Remember, they cannot pass between any
sensors that are switched on.
Turn to the same page as your answer.

Cargo teleporter number forty-six is the correct answer.

Meanwhile, the two masked Blats and Professor Snyde were manoeuvring the trolleys into an observation room. They knew that they were being watched closely by the Blattarian guards, who had obviously been given orders to stay with the trolleys. As they shut the door, they could feel the guards' suspicious glares penetrate their masks. Trying not to look nervous, Snyde passed by the line of guards and began his return journey down the corridor. He hoped that his two friends from BUG were following but he dared not look behind.

He stopped in his tracks when he heard a shout from one of the guards. Turning around, he saw a guard beckoning to the three of them to come back.

'Keep going!' whispered one of the masked Blats from BUG. 'I'll deal with this.'

He returned to be interrogated by the guards. The other masked Blat grabbed the professor's arm and kept walking. As they rounded a corner they began to run. They needed to meet up with the others before the alarm was raised.

Professor Snyde heard a voice speak to him through a speaker in the mask. It was Dajus.

'We can see you on our tracer. We're heading for a cargo teleporter. Meet us en route. You need to take the next left and then the third right and then continue straight through the next three rooms into the corridor. Turn right and we'll meet you in the first room on the right.'

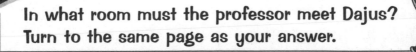

In what room must the professor meet Dajus?
Turn to the same page as your answer.

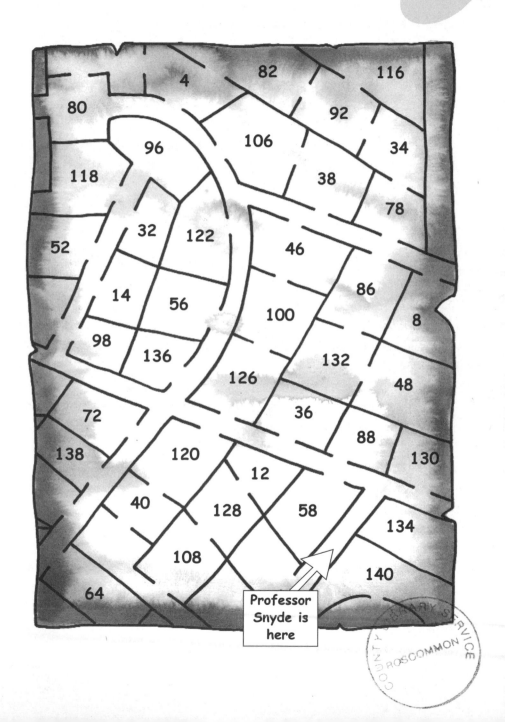

Level forty-eight is the correct answer.

After a few more teleportations, Lisa got used to the process. However, they were now as high as they could go.

'We'll have to go the rest of the way on foot,' said Dajus opening the teleporter door.

Stepping out, Lisa found herself in a long dark corridor. It curved to the right and then disappeared out of sight. Along the right-hand wall were doors but Dajus walked past them all.

'Those doors,' he explained, 'are the private residences of the Blats of level 48. We, however, need to get to Tower Storage on level 56. That is where the humans are being kept.'

Lisa almost had to run to keep up with the long strides of the two Blats. The corridor curved around in what seemed like a large circle. She presumed they were walking the circumference of The Tower.

'This is the maintenance tunnel for this level. It allows workers to make repairs without disturbing the residents or using their teleporters. Each level has one.'

Dajus stopped at a dark archway in the outside wall.

'The maintenance tunnels are connected by ladders which go up and down through shafts in the outside walls of The Tower. The ladders can be reached through these archways but unfortunately I'm not a repair Blat, so I don't know which ladder will take us to level 56.'

He continued walking and very soon passed another black archway into the wall. 'I need a map,' he said, 'and there should be one . . . '

He stopped and peered into the distance.

'Here we go,' he said running ahead.

Lisa and Artox found him at a red cabinet which was mounted on the wall. The cabinet door was open and Dajus was examining a scroll of paper.

'We're on level 48 and we need to get to level 56. I'm just trying to figure out which ladder we should take.'

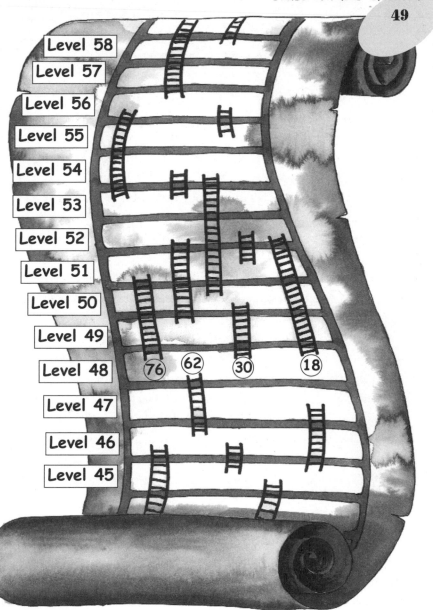

Level 58
Level 57
Level 56
Level 55
Level 54
Level 53
Level 52
Level 51
Level 50
Level 49
Level 48   76   62   30   18
Level 47
Level 46
Level 45

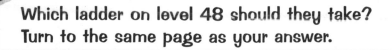

Which ladder on level 48 should they take?
Turn to the same page as your answer.

The skull symbol is the correct answer.

'I don't get it,' Lisa said to Artox.

'What am I?' asked Artox. 'What do I look like to you?'

Lisa paused before answering. Then the puzzle suddenly clicked into place. Artox saw the look of realisation on her face.

'Exactly! A cockroach!'

Without realising it, Lisa turned her nose up.

'Don't even think about it,' warned Artox jokingly. 'After all, you are descended from a monkey, whose roots, if you trace them back far enough, will lead you to the cockroach.'

Artox sat back in his chair and folded both sets of arms. Although you couldn't see his mouth, everything else about him seemed to be smiling.

'Earthlings,' he continued more seriously, 'expose cockroaches by the bucketful to cruel scientific experiments and spend millions of dollars every year trying to exterminate them. And have you succeeded? No! Nor will you ever. Cockroaches are the oldest living thing on your planet. They are 300 million years older than humans. They have watched dinosaurs and thousands of other creatures evolve and become extinct. And they will watch humans become extinct too. When there is nothing left, there will still be cockroaches.

'You see, your cockroaches are survivors. They can live for weeks without food or water. If they can't find water, they take it from the air. If they can't do that, then they just retain it in their bodies. They will eat anything, including each other and humans if necessary. They have become immune to every type of pesticide and can survive an atomic bomb. They have conquered every inch of your planet and have even smuggled themselves into space with your astronauts. They're indestructible!'

Artox stood up to leave.

'Here, read another page.'

Like Earthlings, the people on Blattaria discovered technology. Like Earthlings, they used it to explore space and like Earthlings, they used it to create powerful weapons such as the atomic bomb.

On Blattaria, two countries competed in this arms race. These countries were called Arkendon and Tolcadia. This competition eventually led to war. Arkendon and Tolcadia pulverised each other with atomic bombs. Those that survived the war soon died of radiation. The people of planet Blattaria wiped themselves out in one foul swoop. The air and water was poisoned. All plants and animals died. Everything perished, except for one creature. The Cockroach.

Now follow the cockroach symbol.

Read the above page.
You will be told to follow a symbol.
Turn to the same page as that symbol.

The spade symbol is the correct answer.

'Are you awake?'

Sam blinked his eyes. He must have fallen asleep.

'Are you awake?' came the voice again. It was his fellow prisoner.

'Yes,' groaned Sam, turning to face the wall.

'How are you doing?'

'Fine,' answered Sam even though he wasn't. His head was a mess. He needed to start thinking clearly.

'Tell me more about this Tower,' he said.

'It's almost two hundred floors high and works on a hierarchical system,' whispered the voice. 'Those on the ground floor are those with the lowest status. The higher up The Tower you go, the more wealthy and powerful the Blats are. The government lives at the top.'

'Whereabouts are we?'

'Don't know. Probably somewhere near the top as well.'

'Apart from the government and the guards, who else lives in here?'

'The lucky ones. Everyone else lives in slums and absolute poverty.'

'So how do they decide who gets to live in The Tower?'

'Entry to The Tower is earned. As we speak, Blats are queuing outside waiting to get in. Some have been waiting for years. Entry to The Tower is their reward for loyal service to the goverment.'

'Loyal service?' repeated Sam.

'A nice way of saying that they have all betrayed fellow Blats by reporting illegal activities to the government.'

'What sort of illegal activities?'

'Using technology, stealing food, not cutting your wings, speaking foreign languages or simply speaking ill of the government – they are all illegal activities on Blattaria.'

How long do they queue **FO**r?

When someone dies in The Tower, one Blat from each **L**eve**L** m**O**ves up to the next level creating one free space on the ground floor. They then spend the rest of their lives **W**ai**T**ing to move up to the next level.

Doesn't sound like much of a reward.

You **H**av**E**n'**T** s**E**e**N** **T**he slums

Sssshhh!!! Guards coming!

In the above text are special letters that can be put together.
You will be told to follow a symbol.
To return to Lisa, turn to the same page as that symbol

The eye symbol is the correct answer.

every thing was dark   whirring   electricity

*f*eeling *O*f me*l*ting   drifting   weight *l*essness

b*O*dy separating, dissolving, evaporating

drifting   ap   a   r   t

atoms
  atoms   atoms
      atoms   atoms

atoms
              atoms
    atoms   atoms
     atoms
      atoms   atoms
        atoms atoms
         atoms
          atoms
         atoms
        atoms
       atoms

      planets
     stars   PLANET
    moons
   suns   stars
galaxies   moons
  kilometres   suns
   kilometres   galaxies
    kilometres   space
     billions of kilometres
      PLANET
       PLANET
       PLANET
        PLANET
        PLANET
        PLANET
        PLANET

atoms
atoms atoms
atoms atoms
atoms
atoms
atoms atoms
atoms atoms atoms atoms
atoms   atoms atoms   atoms
atoms   atoms atoms   atoms
atoms atoms atoms atoms
atoms atoms
atoms atoms
atoms atoms
atoms   atoms
atoms   atoms
atoms   atoms
atoms   atoms
atoms atoms   atoms atoms

Whirring   electricity   fusion

joining toge*the*r   again   Solidi*t*y

a feeling   of   weight   b*r*eathing

alive   sound   light   eyes opening

Hidden on these two pages are special
letters that can be put together to tell you
to follow a symbol.
Turn to the same page as that symbol.

Fifty-six seconds is the correct answer.

Having strapped Lisa into her capsule, Dajus prepared to say goodbye. They looked at each other solemnly and Lisa's eyes watered. She realised how lucky she had been. She thought about the BUG members who had risked everything for her, Kreeia, Dajus and especially Artox.

'You know what you have to do when you get there?' said Dajus softly.

Lisa nodded. She felt a trickle down her cheek.

'Thank you,' she whispered.

Her glass cover was closed and she watched Dajus leave the teleporter. She looked at Sam and then at the professor. They too were strapped into their own capsules, waiting.

For a few seconds, time seemed to stop. Everything was still, everything was silent. Reality eventually returned with a gentle hissing noise. Lisa looked down. Her capsule was filling up with green gas. So was the professor's. So was Sam's.

Unlike the last time, the drowsiness was welcomed. She was going to sleep. She was going home . . .

Find a symbol in the picture.
Turn to the same page as that symbol.

Area fifty-eight of the mountain top is the correct answer.

A series of gigantic explosions lit up the sky and shook the whole mountain. Looking out through the trees, Sam saw the satellite dish and teleporter reduced to burning piles of metal. Balls of thick black smoke were released into the clouds. From a distance it must have looked as though the mountain was erupting.

The professor, kneeling, looked a little forlorn gazing over at the scene of destruction. Lisa put her hand on his shoulder.

'It was the right thing to do.'

They had to walk back through the carnage to reach the lift.

'Finish your story,' urged Lisa. 'You were in Dave's office looking for a book . . . '

'Oh yes,' continued Professor Snyde. 'I accidentally knocked over a vase of plastic flowers. The vase smashed and a pile of documents fell out. There were reams of pages written in some kind of coded language. I couldn't figure it out but I did recognise some drawings of the teleporter. Actually, I managed to hold onto a page . . . '

He rummaged in his coat pocket and produced a tattered page. He gave it to Lisa before continuing his story.

'The pages looked suspicious so I e-mailed Dave to come into work immediately. When I showed him the documents he was furious. He swiped them from me and stormed off. By the time I found him again, you two were with him. You probably remember me asking to speak to him.'

The children nodded. They had reached the elevator. The professor hit a button and they heard the elevator grinding to life. As they waited for it to arrive, Lisa examined the curious document.

wew eresurp rise dto he art hat yo uweret heon lyp ersont haty ouw anted tore mainim munef romt hevi rus. wet hough tyo umigh thave fri end sorfa milybu tyo ur wis his ourcom mand. on cet hevirus beg in stos pready oum ust ma kesu re tol iel ow. i fyo uar espot teda sbeingu naffect ed theanti bod ycould beob tained fro myo urgene sand the nourp lanwould beru in ed. on cet hevi rush assp read worl dwi deyoum us tarran gefor ourar rival. fo llowt hebells ym bol

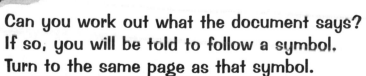

Can you work out what the document says?
If so, you will be told to follow a symbol.
Turn to the same page as that symbol.

Button number sixty is the correct answer.

The Blat kicked Lisa's gear outside the cell and then stood in the doorway. All the time his gun remained fixed on the girl.

'Put those chains on,' he said, motioning to an empty set of shackles on the cell wall.

She moved towards them. She clicked one of the metal rings around her wrist but kept her focus on the Blat. As she clicked the second handcuff, she noticed a shadow behind the guarding Blat. Luckily, he did not.

'Move and I'll kill you,' said a familiar voice outside the cell.

It was Artox! It had worked. Her emergency signal had reached him, and just in the nick of time. She could see the barrel of a gun pointing at Dajus' head.

'Slowly put your gun down,' ordered Artox, 'and step inside the cell.'

The Blat who had claimed he was Dajus obeyed and joined the two children in the cell. Artox stepped into the doorway. Lisa was never so glad to see her Blattarian friend.

'Release the humans,' he commanded, aiming his weapon at Dajus.

'No key,' replied the Blat in a manner which was a little too insolent, considering his position.

As Artox considered his next move, a flash of light suddenly flared outside the cell. Artox's eyes bulged in his head. He dropped his gun and looked at Lisa almost apologetically before collapsing in a heap on the floor. Transparent fluid dribbled out of a hole in his head. He had been shot.

The murderer stepped into the doorway brandishing a smoking laser gun.

It was Sam's Uncle Dave!

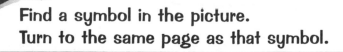

Find a symbol in the picture.
Turn to the same page as that symbol.

The bottle symbol is the correct answer.

When Sam woke up he realised that he was strapped to some sort of bed in a vertical position. He couldn't move his arms or legs, just his head. Lisa was beside him, in a similar state. She was bound to a stretcher that had wheels on the back of it. In front of them was a long table, behind which sat a row of the strange creatures called Blats.

'As you can see,' said a voice, 'I have kept my promise.'

It was Sam's Uncle Dave. He stepped into his nephew's field of vision and addressed the seated Blats.

'Two live, young, healthy human specimens,' he proclaimed. 'Ready for infection.'

The Blats looked at each other and nodded in agreement. Their antennae all touched, as if they were privately communicating with each other. A small Blat at the left end of the table stood up and spoke.

'You have served us well, human, and we too shall keep our promise.'

A Blat two to his left then stood.

'As promised, you shall be spared from infection.'

Another Blat four to his left stood up.

'You will be administered with an antibody to make you immune to the virus.'

A Blat immediately to his right continued.

'Once the virus has spread throughout all of Earth, you will co-ordinate phase two of the colonisation.'

A Blat four to his right spoke next.

'When we have subdued any resistance, a central ruling body will be established to rule the entire planet.'

A Blat three to his left concluded.

'And its leader shall be you.'

Which Blat did not speak?
Turn to the same page as your answer.

Sixty-four is the correct sum of all the equipment.

Back in the control room, Lisa found Artox in discussion with Croy.

'Ready?' he asked.

Lisa nodded.

'It's morning. Time to move.'

As they got ready to leave, all the other Blats crowded into the room to say goodbye to their leader and the strange creature called Lisa.

'Thank you,' she said to the mass of waving claws.

Heading up the passageway, Artox explained the mission.

'If something happens to you, I will continue the mission. If something happens to me, a replacement from BUG will be sent in. If something happens to both of us, then . . . let's hope it doesn't come to that.'

He began to climb the steps to the slum.

'It should be quiet up here now. The Blats will be inside because of the curfew and there will be fewer guards. A Blat's vision is poor in daylight, but don't get too close. Also, watch out for flying patrols.'

Artox put his claw on the metal door.

'I'm going to hijack an air buggy. Do you remember where the teleporter was?'

'Yes.'

'I want you to make your way to it. I'll meet you there.'

Artox opened the door into the little mud hut. The 'word search' lock clicked closed behind them.

'And remember,' said Artox, 'you can reach me or the control room at any time on your micro-com but keep communication to a minimum.'

He moved to the door and looked out.

'I'll see you at the wall surrounding the teleporter.'

And then he was gone. Lisa stepped outside. The sun was just rising. She could see the metal-meshed dome in the distance.

DOME

68 84

90 32

Lisa is here

(g) = guard

Lisa must make her way to the dome without meeting any guards.
What part of the dome does she arrive at?
Turn to the same page as your answer.

Level sixty-six is the correct answer.

Teleporting was now second nature to Lisa and she barely gave it a thought as they were transported up The Tower. She was too busy with other thoughts, thoughts of seeing Sam, thoughts of going home. Looking at Dajus keying in digits on the teleporter keypad made her realise how lucky she had been, how lucky they all had been. Had it not been for Artox and Dajus and the Blattarian Underground Guerrilla, who knows what fate would presently be awaiting them. As her body materialised in a new teleporter, she heard Dajus' voice.

'This is it. The holding cells are on this level.'

The door opened and Lisa stepped out after the Blat. They were in a small enclosure with three doors.

'This is The Tower prison,' said Dajus, checking his weapon. 'The prisoners should still be asleep and the place is seldom guarded – nobody has ever escaped . . .'

He flicked a switch on his gun and a series of small lights lit up.

'If there's trouble of any kind, just hide. Let me deal with the rest.'

He pushed open a door and stepped inside. His insect head looked left and then right. A claw beckoned Lisa to follow.

They were in a small room with two rows of four metal doors on one wall. A narrow stairs and walkway led to the upper row. There were glass windows in each door, all of which were covered in graffiti on the inside.

Dajus seemed to be scanning the cells, as if trying to remember which one was occupied by the human prisoner. Lisa, however, knew at once which cell Sam was in. He had left her a clue, just as he had promised the last time she had seen him.

What number cell is Sam in?
If you have forgotten what Sam said, check back on page 79.
Turn to the same page as your answer.

Person number sixty-eight is the correct answer.

'Well done, you made it,' Uncle Dave said, congratulating the children. 'Now, we must hurry. My truck's over here.'

With the children buckled in, the truck shot off, leaving Rancho El Preson behind as a shimmering blur in the relentless sun.

'There's a couple of things you should know,' said Dave soberly. 'My job is top secret. The location of my work is also top secret and that's the way it must stay. Think you can handle that?'

The children nodded.

'I don't work for the government.'

Lisa looked at Sam.

'I work for a privately funded organisation called SARC – Society for Alien Research and Communication.'

Lisa was full of questions but Dave wasn't her uncle so she waited for Sam to start.

'Aliens?' Sam asked. 'Like little green men aliens?'

'Exactly,' laughed Dave. 'Although we don't think they are green. More like our own skin colour, but paler, or even grey.'

The truck drove towards a tall mountain and eventually pulled up at a high fence with barbed and electric wire running along the top. A sign on the gate said, 'PRIVATE PROPERTY. GUARD DOGS AND CCTV IN OPERATION. KEEP OUT.'

Dave pointed a little remote control at the gate and it opened slowly into a dense forest. The truck sped along a narrow track, turning left at the first junction then taking the next right. It took the second right, ignored the next left, but took the one after that. It went straight at the next junction and then turned right. They were now at the base of the mountain facing a cave.

16   68   60   112   48

At which cave did the truck arrive?
Turn to the same page as your answer.

Room number seventy is the correct answer.

Dave led the kids along a metal balcony that overlooked a large room filled with machines and computers. The place was lifeless except for the low hum and pulsing lights of the technology below. Dave gazed over the machinery like a king surveying his empire.

'What did you mean,' asked Sam, 'when you said that something happened twenty-three years ago that changed your life?'

'I worked for SETI back then. SETI stands for Search for Extra Terrestrial Intelligence . . . '

'Extra Terrestrial? Like ET?'

'Yes. That was our job, searching for aliens. We spent years scanning the stars for radio waves or light beams that might suggest a civilisation other than our own.'

Sam was enthralled. Lisa, however, seemed a little distracted.

'On April 3, twenty-three years ago, I was working the night shift with Professor Snyde and a few others when our photomultipliers detected a series of light flashes emanating from somewhere in the Eagle Nebula. I had waited my whole life for this and honestly thought it would never happen.'

'Was it a message from aliens?'

'It was.' Dave smiled at Sam. He could understand the boy's excitement. All these years later, he still got excited thinking about it.

'What did it say, Uncle Dave?'

'Do you want to see it?'

'Yeah!' shouted Sam, almost choking himself with enthusiasm.

Dave laughed and headed off down the balcony with his eager nephew. But Lisa didn't move. Something was bugging her. Since they had arrived here, she'd had a feeling that they were being followed. Had she just seen something move in the room below? The place certainly seemed empty.

Must have been my imagination, she thought, running to catch up.

Can you see anybody in the picture?
When you're finished looking, follow the leaf symbol.

Fuse number seventy-two is the correct answer.

With the fuse removed, the doors could be forced apart manually. As one of the Blats proceeded to do so, the rest were alerted to an approaching sound. It was the unmistakable tramp of feet. The BUG soldiers raised their guns. One of them uttered something in his own language to Dajus, who replied with a respectful nod.

'Let's go,' he said to the humans and squeezed through a gap in the doors. Two of the Blats followed and the rest stayed to guard the doors.

The hangar was full of air buggies and had a large window leading out into the sky. It was almost night. The three Blats started up a buggy each. Lisa and the professor jumped in behind Dajus. Sam jumped in behind one of the other Blats. Suddenly the air was filled with the sound of shooting. Through the gap in the doors, Sam could see an explosion of light and sparks. He saw a Blat fall but couldn't be sure whether it was a BUG soldier or a Blattarian guard.

Dajus zoomed out the window and shot off into the sky. He was followed by the other buggy and then by Sam's, just as a Blattarian guard squeezed through the gap. Moments later, two buggies appeared in the sky behind them.

There was a gun mounted on the back of Sam's buggy, beneath which were two screens. One showed the night sky and the other displayed a green grid which was marked with numbers on two sides. Beneath the screens was a keypad. As he tried to figure out how to use the device, one of the chasing buggies entered the top screen. It was being driven by a Blattarian guard and was catching up rapidly.

Sam couldn't see a trigger on the gun so he pressed a number on the keypad. Nothing happened. When he pressed another number, however, a laser beam blasted out of his gun. The shot was miles off target but now he realised how to use it. The shot had been aimed at the position given by the co-ordinates – the numbers – that he had entered on the keypad.

TARGET

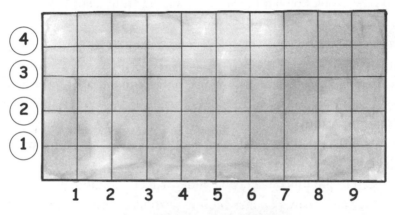

What co-ordinates (two digits) should Sam enter to shoot the approaching buggy? Enter the circled co-ordinate first.

Turn to the same page as your answer.

Blat number seventy-four is the correct answer.

The Blat called Kreeia led Lisa down a passageway to a store room filled with shelves of gadgets and equipment.

'This is a micro-com,' explained Kreeia, holding up a small device like a mobile phone. 'This circular lens is a camera which can be activated by the button on this side. It will relay footage directly back to BUG headquarters. You can also speak to us by pressing a button on the other side.'

Kreeia then took down a metal disc hanging from a string.

'Do you know what this is?'

Lisa looked at the disc's circular face and single hand.

'A compass?'

'Good,' replied the Blat, reaching up for a scroll of paper. 'These are maps of The Tower and its surrounding locality. You never know when you might need them.'

She then pulled down a small backpack and placed the items inside. Lisa slung it over her shoulder.

'You need to put this on as well,' added Kreeia holding out a belt. It had a holster and many pouches on it as well as a series of differently shaped buttons.

'The only button you need to know about is the triangular one. Pressing this will emit an emergency signal to all BUG members in or outside The Tower. Only for emergencies.'

The Blat strapped the belt around Lisa's waist and tightened it. She then produced the final piece of equipment. Lisa knew what it was and didn't want it. Kreeia immediately sensed the girl's reluctance.

'Just in case,' she said, pushing the laser gun into the holster on Lisa's belt. 'Let's hope you won't need it!'

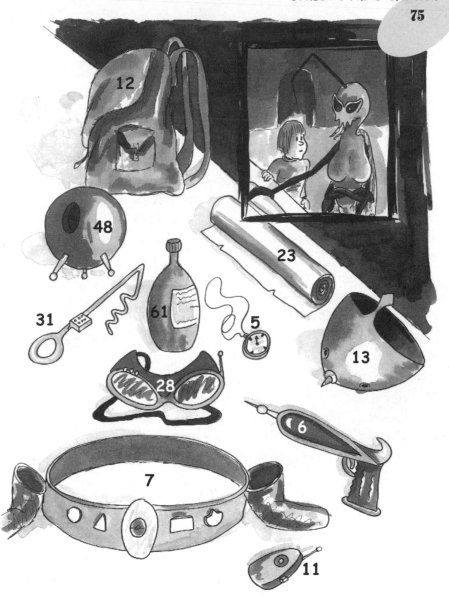

What equipment does Kreeia give Lisa?
Add all the numbers needed.
Turn to the same page as your final answer.

Room number seventy-six is the correct answer.

When they were sure that the guards were not going to enter the room, the ring of protective Blats relaxed their guard. One of them stepped up to Sam and Lisa.

'My name is Dajus.'

Something in Lisa's reaction prompted him to clarify.

'The real Dajus. When The Tower intercepted our plans, they locked me up and sent a fake Dajus to meet you. Luckily I'm not the only BUG spy in The Tower and I was soon released. And just in time, by the looks of things.'

'But how did Professor Snyde get here?' asked a confounded Sam.

'He was teleported here with you. Our plan was to rescue all of you before The Tower even knew you were here but unfortunately we only had time to take the professor. The rest of you were still unconscious. By the time our second rescue team arrived, there was only you left,' he said, looking at Lisa.

'Does The Tower know about the professor?' she asked.

'They knew that an extra body arrived but they didn't really care. It was you two that they really wanted.'

Lisa was still confused but Dajus wasn't waiting around for any more questions.

'We must go,' he urged. 'At any minute they may discover that the two bodies on those trolleys are not human and then they'll be back here straight away. We need to find a teleporter.'

One of the other Blats was examining an electronic claw-held device.

'The floor is heavily guarded,' he said, 'but I think there may be a way.'

Which cargo teleporter can they reach without meeting any guards?
Turn to the same page as your answer.

CT46

CT84

g

They are here

CT74

g

CT20

g = guard

CT = cargo teleporter

The star symbol is the correct answer.

The first thing Lisa saw when she opened her eyes was Sam. He was still in his capsule. Although she couldn't hear him, she knew that he was screaming – and she saw why. Three horrific looking creatures stood around his capsule. They looked like insects but were easily the size of grown men.

They stood upright on muscular hairy legs and each had two pairs of spindly arms. Instead of hands and feet they had sharp claws like those of a crab. One of them stared in at Sam through two huge black eyes. Long antennae, poking out through a metal helmet, gently probed the surface of the glass case.

A second creature stepped forward and pushed the first out of the way. He wore a belt which carried something that could only be described as a gun. What followed seemed to be some sort of angry exchange between the two, although their mouths couldn't be seen. They were hidden under their chins but two little feelers at either side of the mouth moved excitedly up and down.

The third creature stepped in between Sam and Lisa and started to open Sam's capsule from the side. It had a hard shell down its back and two transparent wings hung down over it like a cloak.

When the creature stood back, the glass case was open and Sam's shackles were off. He stared in horror at the three creatures, who seemed just as disgusted by Sam. Gingerly he stepped out of the capsule and edged his way towards Lisa, keeping his eyes firmly fixed on the creatures.

He began to speak but stopped immediately when one of the creatures came towards him. He could only gape at Lisa helplessly, his heavy breathing fogging up the glass of her capsule. Using a finger, he quickly scribbled a message on the clouded glass before two of the creatures grabbed him by each arm.

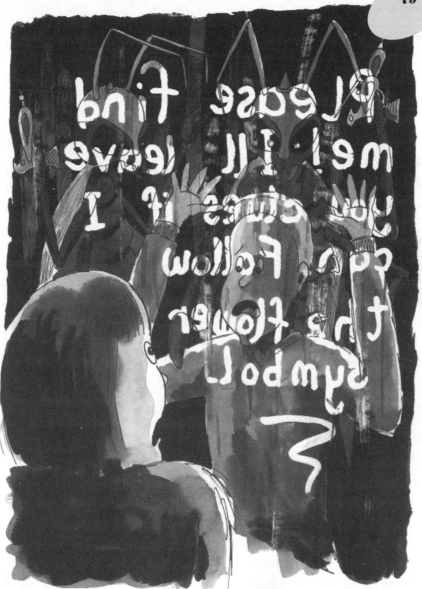

In the message, Lisa is told to follow a symbol.
Turn to the same page as that symbol.

Wire number eighty is the correct answer.

'It's got to be fully destroyed,' reminded Lisa.

'But if it can't be used,' said Sam, who was simply eager to get home, 'isn't that the same thing?'

'No,' she replied. 'It can be repaired, and all it takes is another Uncle Dave and the whole planet is once again in jeopardy.' She realised what she had just said and apologised to Sam.

'It's OK,' he replied. 'As far as I'm concerned, I have no Uncle Dave.'

'If we destroy this,' added the professor, 'he can never return.'

'I know,' nodded Sam, 'but if we don't, we're all in danger.'

Lisa touched him on the arm as a gesture of support, before turning to the professor. 'Will you help us?'

Professor Snyde looked longingly at the teleporter. 'I've spent my whole life working on this and it should pain me to destroy it. But having seen what this did to Dave, and what it could do to the whole human race, blowing it up will probably be my greatest achievement.'

Lisa smiled. 'How will we do it?'

'Dynamite.'

'Dynamite?'

'When we were building this base we used dynamite to blow out rooms and tunnels in the mountain. I remember seeing some in the storage shed.'

He began walking towards a nearby building. The door had already been broken open. Inside they found a whole range of equipment, including sticks of dynamite.

'Find as many as you can,' said the professor.

How many sticks of dynamite can you see in the picture?
Turn to the same page as your answer.

The leaf symbol is the correct answer.

Lisa found Sam and Dave in a room, examining a piece of paper spread out on a table.

'What does it mean?' frowned Sam.

'The message consisted of rapid flashes of light followed by intervals of no light,' explained Sam's uncle. 'This is a numeric printout of the message. It baffled us for a long time but the solution was staring us in the face. Each number of flashes represents a number in our own alphabet. For example, 1 equals A, 2 equals B and so on . . .'

There was a knock at the door. All three heads spun around to find a stern-looking man dressed in a white lab coat staring at them. His long hair framed a hard face with eyes that were dark and menacing.

'Oh . . . Hi Professor Snyde,' stuttered Dave nervously. 'This is my nephew Sam and his friend Lisa. I'm just showing them around . . .'

The professor gave each of them a disdainful glance before fixing his eyes on Dave.

'A word please,' he said coldly and stepped back outside the door.

Dave followed him meekly outside. The professor closed the door. Lisa stepped closer, tuning in to the muffled conversation.

'Don't you understand what top secret means?'

'They won't tell anybody. They're family, just kids.'

'Well you've never cared about family before, why start now?'

'There was nobody else to mind them and . . .'

'Save it! I've more important things on my mind. Come with me.'

Lisa could hear footsteps disappearing down the balcony and then the hiss of an electronic door. Dave popped his head back into the room. His face was flushed but he still managed a smile.

'Be back in a minute, kids. See if you can work out that message!'

He winked at Sam and then closed the door.

'You know, I think I have it,' said Sam, beckoning Lisa over to the table.

Greetings   Earthlings   this   is   a   message
7,18,5,5,20,9,14,7,19   5,1,18,20,8,12,9,14,7,19   20,8,9,19   9,19   1   13,5,19,19,1,7,5

from   another   planet.   We   offer   you   an
6,18,15,13   1,14,15,20,8,5,18   16,12,1,14,5,20   23,5   15,6,6,5,18   25,15,21   1,14

opportunity   to   communicate   with
15,16,16,15,18,20,21,14,9,20,25   20,15   3,15,13,13,21,14,9,3,1,20,5   23,9,20,8

us   but   we   make   certain   conditions.
21,19   2,21,20   23,5   13,1,11,5   3,5,18,20,1,9,14   3,15,14,4,9,20,9,15,14,19.

We   have   been   studying   your   planet
23,5   8,1,22,5   2,5,5,14   19,20,21,4,25,9,14,7   25,15,21,18   16,12,1,14,5,20

for   a   long   time   and   we   know   that   if
6,15,18   1   12,15,14,7   20,9,13,5   1,14,4   23,5   11,14,15,23   20,8,1,20   9,6

this   becomes   public   mass   hysteria   will
20,8,9,19   2,5,3,15,13,5,19   16,21,2,12,9,3   13,1,19,19   8,25,19,20,5,18,9,1   23,9,12,12

ensue.   Therefore   you   must   not   inform
5,14,19,21,5.   20,8,5,18,5,6,15,18,5   25,15,21   13,21,19,20   14,15,20   9,14,6,15,18,13

your   superiors   or   anyone   else.   Instead
25,15,21,18   19,21,16,5,18,9,15,18,19   15,18   1,14,25,15,14,5   5,12,19,5.   9,19,20,5,14

you   must   communicate   with   us   in
25,15,21   13,21,19,20   3,15,13,13,21,14,9,3,1,20,5   23,9,20,8   21,19   9,14

secret   from   a   remote   location   the
19,5,3,20,18,5,20   6,18,15,13   1   18,5,13,15,20,5   12,15,3,1,20,9,15,14   20,8,5

co-ordinates   of   which   are   given   below.
3,15-15,18,4,9,14,1,20,5,19   15,6   23,8,9,3,8   1,18,5   7,9,22,5,14   2,5,12,15,23

If   you   fail   to   meet   these   conditions
9,6   25,15,21   6,1,9,12   20,15   13,5,5,20   20,8,5,19,5   3,15,14,4,9,20,9,15,14,19

you   will   never   hear   from   us   again.   If
25,15,21   23,9,12,12   14,5,22,5,18   8,5,1,18   6,18,15,13   21,19   1,7,1,9,14.   9,6

you   comply   with   our   requests
25,15,21   3,15,13,16,12,25   23,9,20,8   15,21,18   18,5,17,21,5,19,20,19

another   message   will   be   sent   to   these
1,14,15,20,8,5,18   13,5,19,19,1,7,5   23,9,12,12   2,5   19,5,14,20   20,15   20,8,5,19,5

co-ordinates   in   two   years   time
3,15-15,18,4,9,14,1,20,5,19   9,14   20,23,15   25,5,1,18,19   20,9,13,5

14,15,18,20,8   20,23,15   14,9,14,5   23,5,19,20   15,14,5   26,5,18,15.   6,15,21,18

Sam has translated some of the message.
Can you work out what the rest of it says?
There are five numbers mentioned.
Add these five number together.
Turn to the same page as your answer.

The gun symbol is the correct answer.

Sam opened his eyes. He was in darkness. When he tried to move he couldn't. A clinking chain told him why. Around him he could feel nothing but cold stone. Above him was a tiny rectangle of pale light, like a window.

'Lisa?' he shouted into the gloom.

'Shhh!' came a strange voice from the other side of the wall. 'The guards will hear you.'

Sam put his face up to the wall. 'Where am I?'

'You're in The Tower. You're now a prisoner of the Blattarian government.'

'Are you one of them?'

'You mean am I a Blat? Yes, I am the same species. But am I one of them? No, I am their prisoner. You're one of the humans, aren't you? I've seen you on Earth television. In fact, that's what got me here.'

'What do you mean?' asked Sam.

'On Blattaria it's illegal to own or use any technology, including television. Although Blats in The Tower can do whatever they want.'

'But how did I get here?'

'You were teleported here.'

'You mean like in *Star Trek*?'

'Yes. Teleportation is Blattaria's greatest invention. It is the process of simultaneously separating the trillions of atoms that make up a being and then recreating them in the same order elsewhere. Teleporters are used to travel around inside The Tower, around Blattaria and to other planets. Your planet has not discovered how to teleport atoms, although I do believe you have discovered how to do it with photons of light. It's just a matter of time. And after all, we've been around a lot longer than you have.'

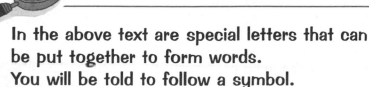

In the above text are special letters that can be put together to form words.
You will be told to follow a symbol.
To return to Lisa, turn to the same page as that symbol.

Room number eighty-six is the correct answer.

The professor found Sam, Lisa, Dajus and the handful of BUG soldiers waiting for them.

'OK the plan is to get you humans airbuggied out of The Tower back to the main teleporter and then back to Earth,' announced Dajus, heading to a nearby cargo teleporter.

Once they had all piled inside it, Dajus hit the buttons and everyone began to disintegrate. Sam was the only one in awe of the process. Nobody else blinked an eyelid, not even Lisa or the professor. They arrived two floors down and flowed out into a corridor.

'The hangar should be just around . . . ' began Dajus before he was silenced by a dreaded sound. A deafening alarm filled the corridor. In fact it seemed to fill the whole tower. It could be heard above, below and all around them.

'They've discovered the bodies!' shouted Dajus, sprinting for the door of the hangar. Everyone else followed but it was too late. The alarm had triggered an automatic lockdown and the hangar doors were just closing as they reached them. Dajus removed a tool from his belt and prised open a metal panel beside the doors. Inside, a web of wires led to a row of fuses.

'The only thing buying us some time,' said Dajus examining it closely, 'is that they don't know where we are. If we remove the correct fuse we can simply cut the power to the door and force it open. However, if we remove the wrong one, we will cut the power to something else. This will show as a fault on The Tower's mainframe computer and will be traced to here – pinpointing our exact location.'

Which number fuse should Dajus remove?
Turn to the same page as your answer.

The tree symbol is the correct answer.

Lisa looked up from the page.

'Your technology,' she said. 'Is that how I got here?'

'Yes, you were teleported here. When our government first sent a message to Earth, it was received by a group called SETI – Search for Extra Terrestrial Intelligence.'

Lisa nodded. She remembered the message.

'The message told the recipients to keep their discovery secret or else there would be no more messages. They were told to set up a secret base at a given set of co-ordinates. The next message would be sent there.'

'SARC,' blurted Lisa. 'The Society for Alien Research and Communication.'

'Yes,' replied Artox. 'The next message sent to your planet contained the first set of instructions for building a teleporter on Earth. The SARC team, headed by some professor, spent the last twenty years or so building it.'

'So why were we brought here?'

Artox pointed to the newspaper.

'The Curse of the Cockroach is being fulfilled: We Shall Inherit All. We have inherited Blattaria, and now we want Earth. Well, when I say "we", I mean the government.'

'You mean, take over Earth?'

'Yes. Their plan is to infect you and your friends with a deadly air-borne disease and send you back to Earth. You would be unaware of the disease and it would remain dormant for a month, before killing you. In that month the disease would have travelled all around your world, wiping out the entire human race. The government could then begin relocating Blats to your planet.'

Artox pointed to the pages in front of Lisa. There was only one more to read.

Eventually the technology on Blattaria became too powerful and too common. Every Blat owned dangerous weapons and soon began fighting each other as individuals, gangs and armies. Blats were about to make the same mistake that humans had made. They were about to destroy themselves.

The government decided to take action. They created a gigantic army called the Blattarian Guard. They then made it illegal for ordinary Blats to own or use any technology. Many wars ensued but eventually the Blattarian Guard gained control of the entire planet.

The Tower was built as a safe haven for the government and all their employees. This is the only place where technology is legal. Everywhere else there is poverty and fear because poverty and fear keeps Blats under control.

There are, however, secret societies that continue to use technology and weapons. Many of these societies have spies inside the Tower who smuggle out technology and weapons and, more importantly, information. BUG (Blattarian Underground Guerrillas) is one such society, and we found out you were coming.

Welcome to Blattaria
Follow the bone symbol.

Read the above page.
You will be told to follow a symbol.
Turn to the same page as that symbol.

Part ninety of the dome is the correct answer.

The place seemed so different during the day. There were no Blats trudging through the streets and there was no smell. There were much fewer guards as well, which made it considerably easier to navigate safely to the dome. Lisa felt very exposed but consoled herself with the fact that, on Blattaria, sunlight was the equivalent to darkness.

At one point, she almost ran into two Blattarian guards coming around a corner. She dived into a doorway but was sure she had been seen. The guards however kept walking and talking in their strange language.

When Lisa reached the high wall of the dome, she looked for somewhere to hide. The ruins of a mud house provided sufficient refuge. Feeling a little more relaxed, she considered her situation. The whole thing was ludicrous. Why did Professor Snyde kidnap them and bring them to this strange place?

And it was a strange place. Although there was night and day, air and clouds, the planet was very different from Earth. There was no vegetation of any sort, no grass, no plants, no trees, no—

Artox's voice suddenly came through the micro-com on her belt.

'Lisa, are you there?'

'Yes,' she whispered into the device.

'I managed to steal an air buggy but I can't collect you, it's too risky. You need to make your way to where I am, on the outskirts of this settlement. Use your compass and follow these directions.'

Lisa fished the compass out of her backpack.

'Go west around the dome. Follow the wall until you can go no further. Then go north. Go west at the third junction and north at the next. Continue to the end of that street and then go east. Go south at the third junction.'

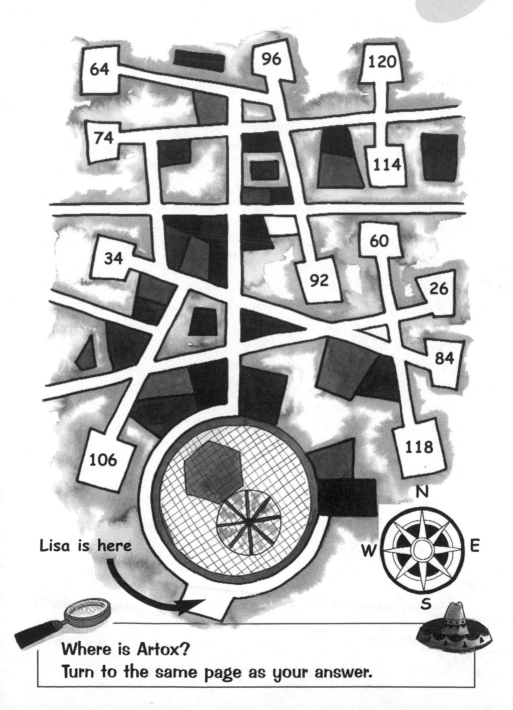

Lisa is here

N

W   E

S

Where is Artox?
Turn to the same page as your answer.

The ghost symbol is the correct answer.

The professor put a finger to his lips and then began loosening Sam's straps. Lisa noticed movement at the other end of the room. The doors of the two large cabinets were quietly opening. Out of them emerged half a dozen Blats armed with assault weapons. Noiselessly they moved across the floor towards her. One of them unstrapped her and she crawled out of her restraints and joined Sam who was now also free.

Bewildered, they watched the Blats continue their operation with military speed and organisation. Each Blat knew exactly what to do and did it soundlessly. The masks were removed from the dead Blats who were then lifted onto the stretchers. Each of them was completely covered with a white sheet. Two of the Blats put the masks on and proceeded to push the trolleys towards the door, the professor leading the way. Before he replaced his own mask, Professor Snyde turned and smiled at the children.

The remaining Blats formed a protective ring around Sam and Lisa and pointed their weapons towards the door. The doors slid apart and the three masked beings walked through, pushing the shrouded trolleys. The Blats protecting the children waited, but nobody entered.

Professor Snyde thought his thumping heart would give the game away as he led the trolleys past the guards waiting outside the door. He could hear them marching behind him. At least none of them had checked the room.

Trace Professor Snyde's route by following the arrows.
To which room does he bring the trolleys?
Turn to the same page as your answer.

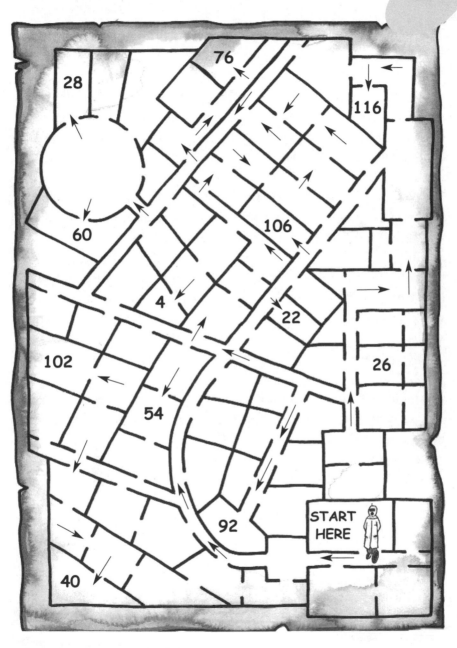

The lightning or thunder bolt symbol is the correct answer.

'Hello?'

'Yes, hello Sam. It's your Uncle Dave here. Listen, Grace has just rung me. The car has broken down and she and your mum won't be back till late. It might even be tomorrow morning. I've been told to come home and mind you.'

'OK.'

'The thing is Sam, I'm actually really busy at work doing something very important, otherwise it would be no problem. How about yourself and Lisa come and spend a few hours at work with me?'

'Sure!'

'Good. OK, you need to take the next bus to Chupadero and get off at Rancho El Preson. I'll meet you there and take you the rest of the way.'

'OK.'

'Good. There's a bus timetable under the phone in my study. See you in a bit!'

And then the line went dead. Sam looked at the phone blankly.

Lisa, who had been eavesdropping, took the phone from him and hung it up.

'Brill!' she exclaimed.

'I don't know why you're so excited. We're just going to be sitting in an office somewhere.'

'Better than sitting here,' said Lisa pulling out the bus timetable. 'What's the name of where we are again?'

'El Pastor'

'And what time is it now?'

'11:50'

BUS TIMETABLE
COLONIA PROGRESO → CHUPADERO

Colonia Progreso	dep.	9:00	12:00	15:00	18:00
El Pastor		9:12	12:12	15:12	18:12
El Mimbre		9:26	12:26	15:26	18:26
Animas		9:42	12:42	15:42	18:42
Rancho El Preson		9:53	12:53	15:53	18:53
Chilicote		10:05	13:05	16:05	19:05
Chupadero	arr.	10:15	13:15	16:15	19:15

How many minutes have they to catch
the next bus?
Turn to the same page as your answer.

Button number ninety-six is the correct answer.

Easing the gate open, Artox and Lisa slipped in. Surrounding the base of The Tower was a line of makeshift huts and tents. They seemed to curl all around it but stopped abruptly at a formidable iron door. Gathered around the door was a group of guards.

Lisa started to speak but was silenced by Artox who was listening to a speaker in his helmet. She could just make out the voice of Croy.

' . . . the password for The Tower is ZAMEN VIX. Nobody enters without it but hopefully you won't need it. One of the Blattarian guards on duty tonight is also one of our own spies. His name is Dajus and he should be waiting for you at the other side of The Tower.'

Artox headed off around the perimeter of The Tower. As Lisa followed, she found it strange that she could see the guards at the door and yet they obviously couldn't see her. She wondered if even Artox saw them.

At the other side of The Tower they found a single guard waiting beside some sort of electric cart.

'You must be Artox,' said the guard, 'leader of BUG.'

'And you must be Dajus,' replied a relieved Artox. They briefly touched antennae before Dajus turned to Lisa.

'And this must be the missing Earthling. Half of the Blattarian Guard is out looking for you.'

Lisa didn't know what to say so she just smiled.

'Any update on the other Earthlings?' inquired Artox.

'Yes,' replied Dajus. 'I can take you to them but we must hurry.'

He pulled back a canvas sheet on the cart. Lisa and Artox clambered aboard before the sheet immersed them in darkness.

A motor hummed to life and the cart moved forward. Lisa could hear the incoherent chatter of the guards getting closer and closer. She held her breath as they spoke to Dajus.

This is the conversation that Lisa heard.
Which speaker is Dajus?
If you don't know, read page 96 again.
Turn to the same page as your answer.

Key number ninety-eight is the correct answer.

As the craft descended, Lisa could make out a barren landscape with crude-looking dwellings, vaguely lit, and thousands of the same strange creatures moving about between them.

Maybe escaping is not such a great plan, she thought.

The vehicle landed rather roughly and Lisa was released by the two creatures, both of whom had discarded their helmets and guns. The taller of the two spoke.

'If a Blattarian guard sees you, you are dead. If anyone else sees you, it will cause such commotion that a guard will quickly find you. Do as I say and don't ask questions. There will be time for that later.'

The creature handed her a bundle of cloth.

'Put this over you and make sure your feet are not seen.'

Lisa complied and found herself in complete darkness.

'Point to where your eyes are.'

She did so and a pointed claw poked two rough holes in the sheet. Lisa could just about see out.

'Follow each street to the end. At the end of the first street turn left. At the end of that street turn right and turn right again at the end of the next one. Then do the same again. So altogether it's left, right, right, left, right, right. Simple. Enter the building at the end of the final street.'

And suddenly they were gone and Lisa was left alone under a grimy sheet. Further up the path she could see creatures moving about, including a guard with a helmet and a gun. Although not at all convinced by her disguise, she began to follow the directions.

As she approached the guard, her heart thumped loudly but she was happily surprised to see another moving sheet up ahead of her. The guard paid no attention to her. It was as if she was a real ghost and not just merely dressed up as one.

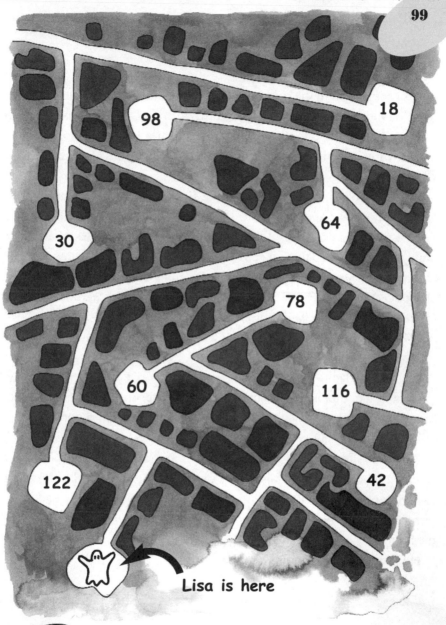

98

18

64

30

78

60

116

122

42

Lisa is here

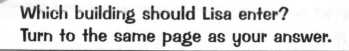

Which building should Lisa enter?
Turn to the same page as your answer.

The apple symbol is the correct answer.

Artox reappeared in the room. 'We don't have much time, but you need to understand some things about us and our planet before we make our next move. One of our Blats prepared that little history lesson for you, to save time. It's in mirror writing for extra protection. How much have you read?'

Lisa showed him and pointed to the line, 'Ask Artox about it.'

The Blat nodded and from a drawer under the table pulled out a bundle of paper. He shoved the top sheet over to Lisa. It looked like a page from a newspaper except that it was written in some strange alphabet. On it, a photograph showed a man dressed in a white coat. He looked odd. His head was unusually large and he had no hair, but other than that he looked quite human.

'This is an ancient Blattarian newspaper,' said Artox. 'We believe you have them on Earth?'

Lisa nodded.

'Of course, this is not the original. The government have that under high security. One of our spies managed to get hold of a copy.'

'What does it say?'

'The headline reads Curse of the Cockroach. The story tells of a scientist who entered his laboratory one morning to find his cockroach experiment gone horribly wrong. All of his cockroaches lay dead in his terrarium. Their bodies were laid out in letters and words to create this message.'

He pointed to a string of strange symbols circled on the newspaper.

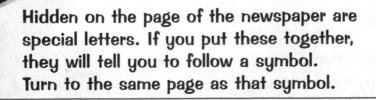

Hidden on the page of the newspaper are special letters. If you put these together, they will tell you to follow a symbol.
Turn to the same page as that symbol.

χυρσε οφ τηε χοχκροαχη

χοχκροαχηεσ! τηεψ ινφεχτ ουρ τρaση χaνσ, λιττερ ουρ ηομεσ aνδ χaρρψ δισεaσε. *f*ωε στeπ ον τηεμ aτ ωιλλ aνδ *O l*σπeνδ a σμaλλ φορτυνε τρψινγ το εξτερμινaτε τηεμ.

μεετ σχιεντιστ μινοοδ χηεaνχ. ηε λιτεσ, εaτσ aνδ σλεεπσ ωιτη χοχκροaχηεσ. ηε ηaσ σπεντ τηε λaστ τωεντψ ψεaρσ στυδψινγ τηεμ aνδ εξπεριμεντινγ ον τηεμ ιν a θυεστ το ιντεντ a ποισον τηaτ τηε ινσεχτσ ωιλλ νοτ βεχομε ιμμυνε το *l O W*.

νορμaλλψ ιτ ωουλδ νοτ *t*βε συρπρισινγ φορ μινοοδ το εντερ ηισ λaβορaτορψ aνδ φινδ ηισ τερρaριυμ φυλλ οφ δεaδ χοχκροaχηεσ. τηaτ ωουλδ υσυaλλψ συγγεστ τηaτ ηισ λaτεστ τοξιχ εξπεριμεντ ηaδ βεεν a συχχεσσ *h e*.

μινοοδ, ηοωετερ, ωaσ συρπρισεδ ψεστερδaψ μορνινγ ωηεν ηε φουνδ ηισ τεστ συβφεχτσ δεaδ.

ι ηaδ φψστ πυτ a νεω βaτχη οφ ροaχηεσ ιντο τηε τερρaριυμ. ι ηaδ νοτ ετεν βεγυν εξπεριμεντινγ

*S*ον τηεμ. ι ωaσ μορε συρπρισεδ το φινδ τηεμ δεaδ τηε νεξτ δaψ βεχaυσε χοχκροaχηεσ aρε *k*ουχη τουγη χρεaτυρεσ.

ωηaτ ωaσ οφ μοστ χονχερν, *U*ηοωετερ, ωaσ νοτ ωηaτ ηaδ κιλλεδ τηεμ βυτ τηε παττερνσ τηaτ τηειρ δεaδ βοδιεσ μaδε ιν τηε τερρaριυμ. *I k*ηεψ λaψ ιν σηaπεσ οφ λεττερσ aνδ ωορδσ τοσ*S* σπελλ τηισ εεριε μεσσaγε*y*:

> ωεσηaλλινηεριταλλ

*M*μaψβε ιτ ωaσ σομε πραχτιχaλ φοκε, *b O*σaψσ μινοοδ, βυτ τηερε ισ νο ετιδενχε οφ aνψ βρεaχη οφ σεχυριτψ. σο τηε νεξτ τιμε ψου στeπ ον a χοχκροaχη, *I*ρεμεμβερ τηειρ προμισε. ψου ηaτε βεεν ωaρνεδ.

The teleporter is number one hundred and two.

'Get down!' commanded Dajus.

Lisa and the professor squeezed themselves down into the back of the buggy. It slowed as it reached the metal-meshed dome that covered the teleporter. Lisa could hear a guard's voice address Dajus but she couldn't understand what he was saying.

The buggy hovered at the gate of the dome as Dajus conversed with the two guards inside. Eventually the metallic grind of the opening gate could be heard and the buggy slowly crawled through.

Once inside, there were two sudden bursts of laser fire, a muffled thud and then silence. Lisa poked up her head to find the two guards slumped motionless in their sentry box. Dajus replaced his gun and manoeuvred the craft towards the hexagonal landing pad. Through the open gate Lisa could see Sam's buggy approaching.

The professor seemed to be glad to be back on solid ground and was the first to jump out. Sam's buggy also landed safely but Dajus seemed concerned.

'We must hurry,' he said, looking up into the sky. 'More guards will come.'

The professor and the children followed Dajus into the teleporter. This was the first thing they had seen on Blattaria and now, hopefully, it would be the last. The three humans stepped into a glass capsule each and prepared to leave.

'How long will the journey take?' asked the professor. The tiny tremble in his voice betrayed his nervousness.

'Well, it takes about eight seconds to be teleported one thousand light years,' answered Dajus, closing his eyes to concentrate. 'We're in the Eagle nebula which is 1,500 light years from the Rosette nebula, which is 300 light years from the Lagoon nebula, which is . . . '

Do we really have time for this? thought Lisa.

How many scoonds will it take to be teleported back to Earth?
Turn to the same page as your answer.

Teleporter number one hundred and four is the correct answer.

Lisa and Artox zigzagged speedily through the minefield of metallic domes. They just reached a teleporter before the entire floor of The Tower was once again alive with flashing sensors. There was no going back now.

'What are all these domes for?' panted Lisa.

'Houses,' replied Artox.

'But where are all the Blats?'

'Inside asleep. Although The Tower receives very little natural light, daytime is simulated by artificial lighting to make sure all Blats sleep when they're supposed to.'

'Doesn't sound much better than the slums.'

'Except that the Blats in here are all fed and watered and free to move about anywhere on this floor and, more importantly, they can strive to move up to level two. They have something to live for. For most of these Blats, this is only the first of many levels.'

Dajus suddenly reappeared and interrupted the conversation.

'Tower teleporters also automatically scan the identities of passengers but luckily this is a cargo teleporter, which means we have unscanned access to all other cargo teleporters in The Tower. Unfortunately, for security reasons, cargo teleporters can only go up five floors or down two.'

He pushed a button on the teleporter and the door slid open. Lisa and Artox followed him inside. The circular chamber reminded Lisa of the last time she had seen Sam.

On a keypad, Dajus keyed in the number of the floor that he wanted to travel to.

They are on floor 1. What floor are they going to?
If you don't know, read page 104 again.
Turn to the same page as your answer.

One, zero, six is the correct code for the elevator.

A few crimson drops on the elevator floor reassured the children that they were going the right way. They dared not think about what was ahead of them. The doors closed automatically and the lift started to move. The elevator display showed an arrow pointing upwards. Eventually the doors reopened – to sky and a gentle breeze. They were outside, on top of the mountain.

Facing them was a gigantic satellite dish. It was perched at an angle, facing the sky like a cereal bowl that had been dropped by a giant. All around them stretched miles of landscape and blurred horizons. But they weren't here for the scenery.

Sam looked around. To his right were three flat-roofed buildings. To his left was another building with some sort of strange machine beside it. The machine was cylindrical with a domed metal roof that sparkled like polished silver. Steps led up to an oval door.

Lisa took a step towards it.

'What do you think is . . . '

Something suddenly cut through the air and Lisa froze, her mouth agape, her eyes widening.

'What is it?' cried Sam glancing frantically around.

Lisa dropped to the ground like a stone.

The sudden sound came again, like something slicing through the air. And then Sam felt it. A sharp piercing pain bit into the back of his leg. He began to feel dizzy and weak. His eyes started to close. He was going to fall. The last thing he remembered seeing, before collapsing into darkness, was a blue dart sticking out of Lisa's back.

From which direction were the darts fired? Turn to the same page as that symbol.

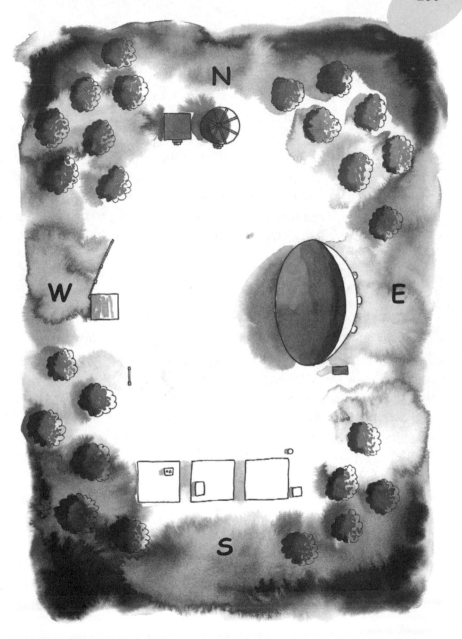

The bone symbol is the correct answer.

'So why did you only rescue me?'

'We wanted to rescue all three of you,' replied Artox, 'but by the time we got there, you were the only one left.'

'What's in this for you?'

'We are naturalists. We don't believe in messing with evolution. If Earthlings are to become extinct, let it happen naturally. Our government has become too powerful. They act like humans instead of Blats. What they're planning goes against everything a Blat should be. We are peaceful creatures. Technology has ruined us as it did humans.'

'So what now?'

'You must return to Earth and destroy the teleporter and this professor.'

'And what about Sam and Dave?' implored Lisa.

'A small price to pay don't you think?' was Artox's reply.

Lisa was abhorred at the idea of leaving Sam and Dave behind. She stood up and eyed Artox doggedly. She could see her determination reflected in his black eyes.

'I don't know what's going to happen,' she stated bravely, 'but I know one thing for sure: I'm not leaving here without Sam or Dave.'

Artox stared at her in silence before rising and leaving the room. It was difficult to sense if he was angry or just disappointed.

Lisa collapsed back into the chair. Her eyes were inevitably drawn back to the ancient newspaper and particularly to the strange curse which was circled. If only she could read it.

She then noticed a piece of card among Artox's bundle of pages. It seemed to be a key for translating the bizarre script from the newspaper into English letters.

abcdefghijk
α β χ δ ε φ γ η ι φ κ

lmnopqrstu
λ μ ν ο π θ ρ σ τ υ

vwxyz
ϖ ω ξ ψ ζ

ωεσηαλλινηεριταλλ

Translate the curse into English.
How many words are in the curse?
Turn to the same page as your answer.

Cell number one hundred and ten is the correct answer.

Dajus opened the cell door to reveal Sam asleep on the floor with his arms manacled to the wall. Lisa dashed inside and fell to her knees beside him.

'Sam! Sam!' she whispered, shaking him gently.

He flickered open his eyes to find the face of his best friend smiling down at him.

'We've come to rescue you!' cried Lisa excitedly.

'Wrong!' said a voice behind her. It was Dajus and he was pointing his gun at her. 'Your boyfriend here was merely the bait to catch the fish that got away.'

'But Dajus . . . ' began Lisa in bewilderment.

'I'm not Dajus!' snapped the Blat. 'All I had to do was look like him and you walked straight into our trap.'

Lisa was speechless.

'One of our spies in BUG tipped us off – yes, we have spies too,' laughed Dajus. 'Getting you in here was entirely staged to make things look authentic. Do you honestly think it would be that easy to get into The Tower?'

The colour had drained from Lisa's face. She felt like someone had kicked her in the stomach.

'Slowly take off your belt and backpack and slide them over here,' commanded the Blat, pointing towards her belt with his gun. 'Any sudden moves and I'll shoot.'

Lisa slid off her backpack and pushed it across the floor. As her fingers fumbled along her belt to find the buckle, they detected the series of buttons. She then remembered something that Kreeia had said to her back in BUG headquarters.

The Blat never even noticed her pressing the button before she unfastened the belt and slid it across the floor.

Which button did Lisa press?
If you can't remember what Kreeia said,
check back on page 74.
Turn to the same page as your answer.

Cave number one hundred and twelve is the correct answer.

Another press of the remote control opened a gate into a cave with strip lighting. The truck rolled quietly into a concrete car park deep under the mountain. A van with tinted windows sat lonely in one corner.

'But I was sure you worked for the government,' said a puzzled Sam clambering down out of the vehicle.

'I did. I worked for NASA and subsequently SETI but twenty-three years ago something happened that changed my life and caused me to leave. Myself and a small team of devoted colleagues left and set up SARC and this top secret research centre.'

The children followed Dave to a metal door. Inside, concrete steps led upwards.

'Private funding from wealthy benefactors has put us years ahead of any government operation,' panted Dave as he ascended the stairs.

The stairway was dark and steep, with rough damp walls that had been brutishly cut from the rock.

'But sometimes,' he continued jokingly, 'I think the budget could have stretched to an elevator.'

Lisa turned around and peered back down the steps. She could have sworn that she heard the metal door that they had just come through open and close. She squinted down into the gloom. Nothing but shadows. She shook her head and hurried up the steps after the other two.

After much climbing and many turns, the children reached their destination, weary but intrigued.

At which room did they arrive?
Follow the arrows to find out.
Turn to the same page as your answer.

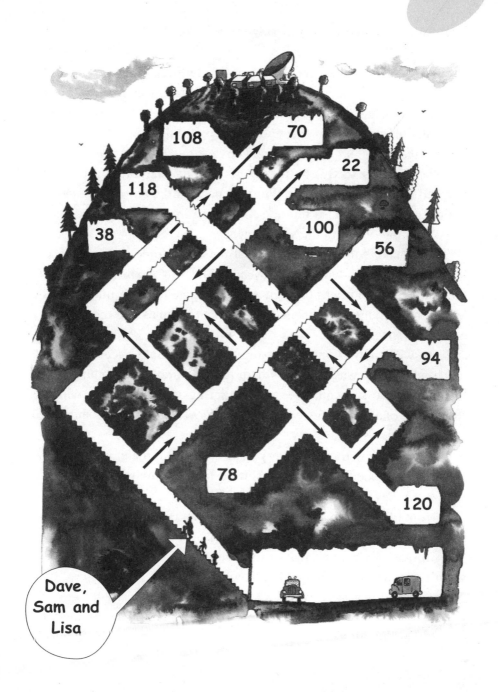

Artox is at location one hundred and fourteen.

Crouching, Lisa made her way along the derelict streets, eager to be reunited with the leader of BUG. She found him sitting in an air buggy, wearing a Blattarian Guard helmet. The buggy was like the one she had been in a few hours ago, except that this one didn't have a cage.

'Into the back,' urged Artox, 'and cover yourself.'

Although not exactly chuffed about the idea, she didn't protest and crawled in under the pile of cloth in the back of the buggy. The vehicle hummed softly and Lisa felt herself rise up into the air. She couldn't resist peeking out from under her sheet.

Below, she could see the metal-meshed dome containing the teleporter, her only way off this planet. She was again reminded that the only way into it was through an armed gate in the roof. The dome and its surrounding settlement quickly became smaller as the air buggy picked up speed.

They were now flying over barren land, desolate except for sand, mud and rock. It was a desert where nothing grew and nothing lived. In the distance she could see a meandering valley, through which a river must once have flowed, but which now looked like a shrivelled snake, dusty and dead.

They were now travelling very fast, the wind threatening to lift the sheet. Lisa gripped it tightly and shifted her position so that she could see where they were heading.

In front of them was an enormous mountain rising up out of the sand and towering into the clouds. It was a bizarre sight, as there were no other mountains nearby. It was more like a . . . Lisa realised that it wasn't a mountain. This was The Tower.

'Get down!' warned Artox, looking back at her. 'Guards!'

Lisa ducked down, seconds before she was surrounded by the hum of many air buggies.

In which air buggy is Lisa?
Turn to the same page as your answer.

The bell symbol is the correct answer.

Once inside the lift, the professor continued his story.

'I wanted to speak to Dave somewhere more private, so I asked him to my office. As we headed there, he hit me over the head with something hard. I passed out and eventually woke up in that storage shed on top of the mountain. I had lost a lot of blood but I was OK. The shed was locked but I managed to escape just in time to see you two being shot with tranquilliser darts. Dave carried both of you into the teleporter so I followed. By the time I got there, the three of you were secured in teleporting pods and already unconscious from the gas. The teleporter was on a timer and couldn't be stopped. Before I could get out, the door sealed and I was trapped inside. The countdown for Earth's first teleportation had begun. I quickly strapped myself into an empty pod which filled up with gas. The four of us were then teleported to Blattaria.'

'But how come we never saw you?' frowned Sam.

'I received a smaller dose of gas because I was late into my pod and so I was first to wake up. A group of Blats who later turned out to be the Blattarian Underground Guerrilla rescued me. During our escape the rescue team lost their micro-com and couldn't communicate back to BUG headquarters. By the time the second rescue team arrived, only Lisa was left. My rescue team knew Sam had been captured so they smuggled me into The Tower to help him escape. I guess you know the rest . . . '

They left the lift and made their way down many stairs and tunnels until they arrived at a door in the underground car park.

At which door did they arrive?
Turn to the same page as your answer.

Blat number one hundred and eighteen is the correct answer.

The final Blat to speak stood up.

'The two subjects shall now be infected and immediately returned to Earth to spread the virus. Take them away.'

Some Blats approached the children and manipulated their stretchers into horizontal positions. They were then both pushed out of the room by a team of guards.

Sam's mind was in turmoil. As he sailed past the white lab coat of his uncle, he tried to say something but the words stuck in his throat. Before he knew it he was out of the room and travelling briskly down a long corridor. He could hear Lisa's trolley rattling behind him.

They passed many doors on both sides but eventually the corridor curved around to the left and they entered a door at the end of it. They passed through a square room and into a short corridor. The first door on the left took them into a large bright area where they were parked under two white lights. The guards then marched out of the room and the electronic doors hissed closed behind them. Sam and Lisa were left alone in silence.

The room was completely white and immaculately clean. There were two large metal cabinets like giant wardrobes up against one wall. Opposite them on a bench, little bottles and tubes of coloured liquid stood among highly technical-looking scientific equipment. Two computer screens on the wall were like watchful eyes. Above them hung stainless steel instruments including blades and scissors. It didn't take much imagination to guess what they were for. More alarmingly, however, was what lay in between the two children. Two syringes were filled with a transparent liquid. Their glinting needles pointed in opposite directions, one towards Sam and the other towards Lisa!

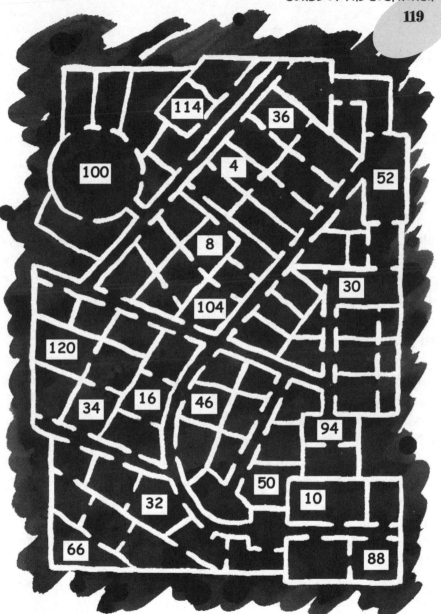

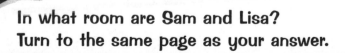

In what room are Sam and Lisa?
Turn to the same page as your answer.

The flower symbol is the correct answer.

Lisa watched despairingly as her best friend was dragged out the door by the gruesome beasts. Alone now in her glass cage, she contemplated her own fate. She knew they would be back for her. Scanning the other glass capsules, she saw that they had already taken Sam's uncle.

Poor Dave, she thought, and poor Sam. Her thoughts were about to turn to 'poor me' when the door of the room re-opened and two more giant bugs marched in. She braced herself as they approached. Four black eyes gaped into her capsule while their antennae moved searchingly across it. Lisa could see her petrified face reflected in the four dark eyes. Then she noticed movement behind the two beasts. Two more creatures had entered the chamber, unbeknown to the first two. Although similar to the others, these wore no helmets, had much shorter wings and carried larger guns.

Simultaneously, they raised their weapons and pointed them at Lisa. She scrunched her eyes closed but even through her eyelids she saw the flash of lights and felt the thud as something hit her glass case.

When she opened her eyes, she found the two helmeted creatures lying dead on the floor. A colourless fluid dripped down the outside of the capsule. The two attackers quickly removed the helmets from the corpses and put them on themselves. They then turned their attention to the capsule. In seconds the door was open and her shackles prised apart.

Lisa was about to scream when a soft voice said, 'Do not be afraid. We are here to help you but you must hurry. Follow me.'

The two creatures disappeared out of the room. Lisa followed them out the door and onto a hexagonal platform.

88

20

74

50

66

24

26

4

54

12

82

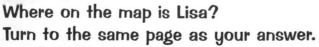

Where on the map is Lisa?
Turn to the same page as your answer.

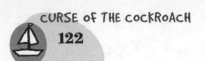
The boat symbol is the correct answer.

Sam awoke. It took him a few minutes to realise he was in the teleporter. The question was, were they still on Blattaria or were they back on Earth? Lisa was coming to, as was the professor.

The glass case surrounding the boy suddenly clicked and slid to one side automatically. His ankle and wrist restraints also clicked apart. Feeling a little dizzy, Sam stepped from his pod and headed for the door. The other two could wait. He pushed a panel on the door and it swung open.

He was greeted by a fresh breeze, clouds and a giant satellite dish. He was on top of the mountain! He was home! Well, almost. Turning around he saw that Lisa and the Professor had been released from their capsules too.

The three of them stood in silence outside the teleporter door, savouring the view, inhaling the wind.

There's no air like Earth air, thought Sam smiling.

Lisa however wasn't getting carried away.

'We're not safe yet,' she warned, addressing Professor Snyde. 'The teleporter must be destroyed.'

The professor looked a little shocked. Lisa knew that he had put his life into this project, as had Sam's uncle.

'They could be teleporting the virus as we speak,' she continued.

The professor knew she was right and walked briskly around to the side of the machine. He removed a panel on the side to reveal a mesh of wiring.

'If we cut the wire connecting the stabiliser to the quantum entangler, then nothing can be teleported here. At least it buys us some time until we figure out what to do.'

Which number wire should they cut?
Turn to the same page as your answer.

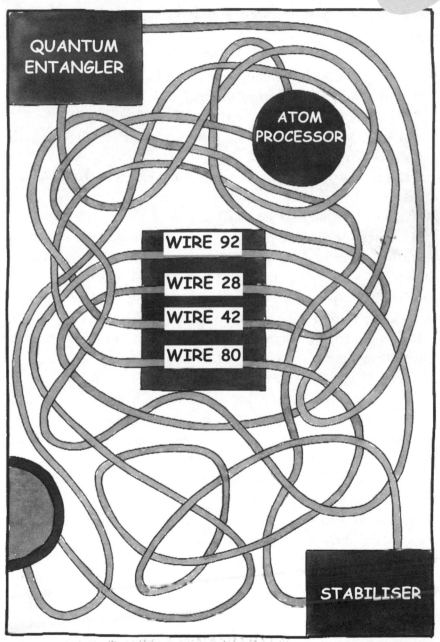

Door number one hundred and twenty-four is the correct answer.

Sam and Lisa buckled themselves into the back of the professor's van.

'Where to?' he asked, starting the engine.

'Do you know where my Aunt Grace lives?' replied Sam.

'Oh I do,' smiled the professor, his eyes twinkling slightly in the rear-view mirror.

Strange, thought Sam, but he was more concerned about his Aunt Grace.

'What will we tell her?' he asked in panic.

'The truth,' replied the professor, 'and I think you'll find that she won't be too upset about your Uncle Dave. You see, behind all his smiles and jokes, your uncle was quite a nasty man and he was particularly nasty to your aunt. It was only a matter of time before she left him. We were waiting for the right time . . .'

He stopped talking and put the van in gear. A red love heart with the letter G embroidered in gold thread swung crazily from the rear-view mirror as the van bounced along the forest track.

The professor popped a CD into the stereo. The unmistakable sound of Kurt Cobain unplugged filled the interior of the van.

Wouldn't have put him down as a Nirvana fan, thought Lisa smiling to herself.

It was only then that she realised which song was playing – 'The Man who sold the World'.

She closed her eyes and let the lyrics drown out everything else. Indeed she had come 'face to face with the man who sold the world', but she had bought it back.

THE END

Page	Answer	Page	Answer	Page	Answer	Page	Answer
2-3	42	34-35	62	64-65	90	94-95	22
4-5	14	36-37	54	66-67	110	96-97	44
6-7	48	38-39	106	68-69	112	98-99	18
8-9	52	40-41	66	70-71	82	100-101	50
10-11	92	42-43	94	72-73	28	102-103	56
12-13	96	44-45	104	74-75	64	104-105	6
14-15	74	46-47	86	76-77	46	106-107	36
16-17	38	48-49	30	78-79	120	108-109	4
18-19	32	50-51	20	80-81	26	110-111	60
20-21	84	52-53	12	82-83	16	112-113	70
22-23	68	54-55	78	84-85	88	114-115	8
24-25	98	56-57	122	86-87	72	116-117	124
26-27	58	58-59	116	88-89	108	118-119	10
28-29	102	60-61	34	90-91	114	120-121	24
30 31	40	62-63	118	92-93	76	122-123	80
32-33	100						

Also from Kieran Fanning

Trapdoor to Treachery

Sam and Lisa decide to do some investigating when a series of mysterious thefts plagues their town. Following the trail of the thief, they are led into a strange and exciting world full of puzzles, elves and gobbledegooks. They must take care, however, as danger lurks around every corner.

'**Excellent entertainment.**' *The Sunday Tribune*

Voyage to Victory

When a school trip to a museum gets interrupted by a security alert, Sam and Lisa are somehow transported back in time to the eighth century. They suddenly find themselves in the clutches of a band of ferocious Vikings on a quest to steal the most valuable artefact in the world. Sam and Lisa's only hope of escape lies with this precious object. Their hunt for it takes them on the most amazing adventure to distant worlds where they encounter fearsome Viking gods, an eight-legged horse and many other strange and wonderful creatures.

'**Inventive, stimulating, provocative – a must.**'
Sunday Independent

Tempest of Trouble

The trouble starts at school when Sam and Lisa's new teacher turns out to be an evil witch! Using her magic wand and weird ingredients, Miss Sycorax casts one diabolical spell after another. Before they know it, Sam and Lisa find themselves stranded on an enchanted island with this vengeful witch, her wart-infested son and a host of enslaved sprites and whispering ghosts. Their only hope of escape is to banish the dreaded Sycorax.

'**A busy, active and very enjoyable journey.**' *Irish Times*

**To write a review, contact the author,
read extracts and more, visit
www.kieranfanning.com**